THE
SECRET
SIDE
OF
EMPTY

THE
SECRET
SIDE
OF
EMPTY

MARIA E. ANDREU

RP|TEENS
PHILADELPHIA · LONDON

Books published by Running Press are available at special discounts for
bulk purchases in the United States by corporations, institutions, and
other organizations. For more information, please contact the Special
Markets Department at the Perseus Books Group, 2300 Chestnut Street,
Suite 200, Philadelphia, PA 19103, or call (800) 810-4145, ext. 5000, or
e-mail special.markets@perseusbooks.com.

ISBN 978-0-7624-5192-0
Library of Congress Control Number: 2013950819

E-book ISBN 978-0-7624-5205-7

9   8   7   6   5   4   3   2   1
Digit on the right indicates the number of this printing

Cover images: Bicycle scene © Thinkstock/Oleg Podzorov;
Girl © Shutterstock/Andrei Aleshyn
Designed by Frances J. Soo Ping Chow
Edited by Lisa Cheng
Typography: Adobe Caslon, Abraham Lincoln,
Quicksand, and Samantha

Published by Running Press Teens
An Imprint of Running Press Book Publishers
A Member of the Perseus Books Group
2300 Chestnut Street
Philadelphia, PA 19103–4371

Visit us on the web!
www.runningpress.com/kids

For Pablo,

We made it.

For Andreanna and Zachary, my A through Z,
my beginning and my end.

My everything.

CHAPTER ONE

"You're a menace to pedestrians everywhere. I hope you know that," I say, looking back at the old lady whose toes Chelsea just narrowly missed crunching.

Chelsea laughs, tosses back her head, and waves her right hand at me in cheerful dismissal. I notice two things. One is the delicate charm bracelet that jingles on her right wrist, with its little bejeweled soccer ball charm her dad got her the other day, just because. The second is that her hands still look so much like the way they did that first day in kindergarten, all thin fingers, delicate, pale, long. I wonder if generation after generation of living in big houses and having everything makes people prettier somehow, maybe a good nutrition, superior genes thing.

I put down the visor to check out my eyeliner. Chelsea's cousin Siobhan and I make eye contact for a split second. She looks away first, but by a short moment. Awkward. I check her out for an instant longer.

You can see the family connection between her and Chelsea: same snub nose, same skin that looks like a few layers have gotten rubbed off and it's just not thick enough to hold in all her veins and guts and stuff. On Chelsea, it's angel pink. On Siobhan, it's blotchy. Chelsea's perfectly athletic supermodel height has also not made it across the cousin lines. Siobhan is short and stubby, and seems a little irritated by the ticket she's drawn in the genetic lottery.

Siobhan says, "Anyway, so then it turns out it's not just regular twin sheets, as if it's not bad enough I have to sleep on a twin bed, which I haven't done since . . . I don't think I've ever done, actually . . . it's not just a regular twin, it's, like, some freakishly long twin, so all the sheets my mom picked up at the mall don't even fit. So we had to go exchange them to get this special college length, and they had *nothing* cute in that weird size. Nothing." She stops to let the true horror of that fact sink in. No. Cute. Sheets. She may just need to rethink this whole college thing with a catastrophe like that looming.

I think—not for the first time—that Siobhan needs more bad things to happen in her life. Not that I'm wishing her ill, exactly, but I think she needs something to put her life in perspective. If not personal hardship, maybe a trip to Malawi might even do the trick.

"And, I don't know, I mean, I guess I'll have to wait and see until I meet them, but my roommates sound like weirdos."

Chelsea seems to actually like her cousin. This baffles me. She asks, with real concern in her voice, "Why do you think so?"

"I mean, one is from, like, Alaska. Some kind of hunting bizarro chick, maybe? Who knows? And the other one . . . Margarita Perez or something. Some Spanish kid, from, like, the Bronx. Who will probably be selling drugs right out of our dorm room. Either way it sounds like they'll both be packing heat."

Chelsea glances over at me for about three nanoseconds, then away. That look tells me that she doesn't want me to make a thing of it. "Oh, Siobhan. You *know* M.T. is Spanish."

You can tell that if she once knew, she has long since forgotten, like all other unpleasant facts in her life.

"But you don't look Spanish," says Siobhan.

I fight back the urge to say, "What does 'Spanish' look like?"

I guess I don't look like what most people think of when they think of Spanish, if they think of it at all. I'm pale white and I've got blondish hair, which I sometimes help along with a little lemon juice. Which eventually turns it into a split-ends mess, but, oh well. Because, yeah, some people who speak Spanish are also white. When people try to guess my nationality (and you'd be surprised how often that is), I get everything—Greek, Italian, Russian, Croatian. I am like the blot test of heritage. Ukrainians see Ukrainian. Poles see Polish. Italians invariably see Italian.

"Yeah," Siobhan says, recovering, but not well. "I mean, I don't mean, I mean, you're like . . . what, like . . . a genius, right? Rooming with you would be fine, right? It actually has nothing to do with, like, where anyone's from, like, originally. Just, the Bronx, you know?"

"No, I get it," I say. I don't get it, but I don't want to keep watching her turn this alarming shade of red, either, and I don't care enough to start something over it. I'm not proud enough of the whole "Spanish" thing to take up the fights of "my" people. I kind of hate it, actually.

Siobhan looks relieved that she averted a Racial Incident, the kind she's heard about on some MTV reality show. I turn back to the road and try to focus on the fun side of the afternoon.

Despite the fact that Chelsea is a terrible driver, I love hanging out in her car. And not just because it's a BMW 3 Series in a beautiful pewter, with a sunroof I could play with all day. It's more that adventures always seem cooler when they're moving. We are in the next town over from Willow Falls, a town that actually has a decent strip. A lot of kids drive up and down between the diner on one end and the Ann Taylor store at the other end, so we almost always run into someone we know. Sometimes we park and walk it, but today we cruise, listening to bad music on the radio and keeping cool in the AC.

Siobhan goes back to safer ground: the college thing. "Yeah, anyway, so it's a good school. They have so many great classes in my

THE SECRET SIDE OF EMPTY

major. I think it was those internships that really paid off, you know? That and the SAT classes. It was nice to get into an Ivy, but I think a smaller school is just a better environment for me, you know? And plus, when I went on the visit, everyone seemed so friendly."

The *War and Peace* of college decisions, this one. She made it months ago, but she's still reliving it, like she's got college decision post-traumatic stress syndrome.

Finally, it seems like Siobhan may be getting the clue that she is only talking about herself, so she changes the subject to include other topics, like what *we* think about her new college.

"I mean, you should definitely come up and check it out," she says, looking at Chelsea. "You could have a great time there, and they have a great sports program. You should talk to some of the coaches."

It's weirdly quiet for a second.

"Oh, and you too, of course . . . *M.T.* . . ." She still stumbles over my "new" name, because the last time she came east to stay a week with Chelsea's family, we were still in eighth grade and I still went under my full name, not my initials. You can tell she doesn't approve, but she doesn't have the guts to say so. But I can imagine she's also glad she doesn't have to try to pronounce my real name.

"Yeah, that would be awesome," says Chelsea. "We should

definitely go, M.T. You think your parents would let you spend a weekend up there? I could drive. Road trip!" She stares at me way longer than any driver should take her eyes off the road, so I feel obligated to stop this little college-visit train.

"Yeah, I'm actually . . . I think I'm not going to college." I've been meaning to drop this on Chelsea for a while, ever since she started taking weekend visits and SAT prep courses junior year.

"What!" she says, but it shocks her enough to look back at the road. "Oh. Very funny. Haha. Is it that you want to go to a bigger school? With your grades you should be able to get in anywhere."

"Yeah, college, I mean, who cares, right? More indoctrination, being told what to read and what to think. I think I want to get out there and live, you know what I mean?"

Even I don't know what I mean, but I think I put on a pretty convincing performance. I mentally pat myself on the back for using a big word when lying about not wanting any more education.

Siobhan is sputtering. I have just blown up her world. "I don't understand," she says. "Are you talking about traveling around for a year or something? Doing the backpacking-through-Europe thing? Deferring enrollment? A gap year?"

"I'm talking about not going to college," I say.

While Siobhan is still sputtering in shock, a car full of boys pulls up next to us. They hold up McDonald's bags to the windows and make weird faces at us.

"Who are those guys?" says Siobhan. "Do you know them?"

"The driver plays in my brother's tennis league. None of the other ones looks familiar," says Chelsea.

"Isn't that Sarah's old boyfriend in the back?" I ask.

Chelsea squints and looks at them. "Mmmm . . . maybe? He looks familiar, yeah."

The driver rolls down the window and says something. They're on my side, so I roll down my window.

"My friends just bet me I couldn't throw a fry and have you catch it."

"Your friends are going to win that bet because I am not a trained seal," I say. His friends all laugh.

"We'll give you a present!"

"Chels, green light, take off!" says Siobhan. Chelsea guns it. The boys race to catch up, weaving past other cars until we get to another red light next to each other.

"We have soda!" says one in the back.

I turn to Chelsea. "Soda is intriguing. I'm kind of thirsty."

Chelsea calls back in her best flirty voice, "We'll take soda, but there will be no fry catching."

Everyone but the driver gets out of the car and comes over to ours. In the middle of the street. One of them—a cute one with big, dark green eyes—carries two Sprites and an energy drink. I roll down the window and take them, then hold up the energy drink. "Do we look lethargic?" I say to him.

He smiles, and it's like lamps have been turned on in his eyes, lighting up his whole face.

"It's what we've got," he says.

The light turns green and his friend takes off driving. They all run after the car.

Chelsea giggles. "The driver is kind of cute."

"I like Soda Guy."

"Yeah, he was totally checking you out. But let's make this interesting for them," says Chelsea, turning off the main drag, then driving fast a few blocks ahead and coming on to the strip going in the opposite direction.

We drive about a block until they pass by us, going the other way. All their windows open up and one of the guys pops out of the sunroof. "How did you guys get over there?" screams the driver. Chelsea shrugs and smiles and accelerates a little too fast.

"Oh my God, Chelsea!" says Siobhan from the backseat, the "oh" a little scream. I hear screeching tires. The guys have done a U-turn and are behind us again. At the next red light, they pull up.

The driver hangs out his window. "You trying to lose us?"

"Honey, if I was trying to lose you, you'd be lost," says Chelsea.

A chorus of boys say, "Ooooh," at the challenge.

"Yeah?" says the driver. "Let's see."

I'm disappointed, because I want more excuses to talk to Soda Guy. Where is the fun in losing them?

Chelsea switches into NASCAR mode, peeling off the main strip at the next light. She blazes through a red light and, surprisingly, the boys don't follow. Chelsea makes one turn, then another. I think we've lost them, but when I turn around, I see them about a block behind us.

"They're still following us!" yells Siobhan.

"Not to worry," says Chelsea, making another right, then a left, then a right and . . . turning right into a dead end.

Before Chelsea can put the car in the reverse, the boys pull up and block our exit. And all get out of the car and walk toward ours.

"Lock the doors! Lock the doors!" says Siobhan.

"Relax, they're just playing around," I say.

They stand around our car, like now that they've caught us they don't know what to do.

"Come out," says Soda Guy, standing by my window now, mouthing the words in an exaggerated way. I get a better look at him. He's got messy brown hair and glasses I hadn't noticed before.

I jerk my head in Siobhan's direction and shake my head. "I can't," I say.

"We won't bite," he says, making a chomping motion with his hand.

I open the window about a dime's width.

Siobhan screeches from the backseat, "Are you crazy?"

"Hey, see, that wasn't so bad, right?" he says.

I smile.

"Are you from Oakberg?"

"Willow Falls."

"Yeah? I've never seen you at school," he says.

"That's because I don't go to Willow."

"Ooooh, mysterious. So are you, like, a girl genius who finished college at seven? Are you now practicing medicine?"

"Something like that."

I hear Chelsea giggle at something Tennis Guy just said to her.

Siobhan is getting more frantic by the minute. "Chelsea, there is a lady looking at us from her porch over there." Siobhan is seriously so annoying. But it's not Chelsea's fault. You can't judge people by who they're related to. I am the poster child for that.

"We're cornered and we're late," I say to Soda Guy. "Can you offer assistance?"

He scrunches his nose and tilts his head to one side.

"I think it would be more fun if we could talk for a while longer," he says.

I hear Tennis Guy and Chelsea discussing the logistics of a good drag race. Tennis Guy is clearly into Chelsea. But then most guys are. Another one of the guys in the car nudges the back of the car a little. Siobhan jumps.

"We really have to get home," I say to Soda Guy.

He nods. "Okay, maybe next time?"

I nod.

He nods again. For a second it's awkward, the two of us bobbing our heads at each other and him not moving. Finally, he says, "Mission accepted. I'll get them out of the way for you." He grabs another guy by the shirtsleeve, whispers something in his ear, and they head over to Tennis Guy's car. Suddenly I hear the car peeling out of the dead end in reverse.

Tennis Guy and the other guy realize their friends are driving off with the car and leaving them behind. They start screaming at them and sprinting after the car. The coast is clear. The lady Siobhan had pointed out to Chelsea is still staring at us. There is a little kid standing next to her, kind of behind her leg. She motions to me, so I roll down the window a little more.

"I didn't know what those guys were up to, so I called the cops. Are you guys okay?" she says. I nod at her, but my heart starts to pound.

Cops. I can't do the cop thing. "Chels, let's go home," I say.

"We're fine," Chelsea calls out. "Tell them it was just a crazy teenage mating ritual!"

The woman shakes her head at us. Siobhan punches Chelsea in the arm. I sigh in relief when Chelsea guns it out of there.

CHAPTER TWO

An army of Central American men with big machines strapped to their backs are swooshing away every leaf on the unnaturally green lawns that I am biking past. These Guatemalan and Mexican men—that's who people around here think of when they think "Spanish."

They know better than to pigeonhole and stereotype, the residents of this fine suburb. They're college educated. They've got some stamps on their passports. They know about South America and Central America and Spain and all that stuff. But these guys and the women who keep the inside of their houses spotless and their kids' diapers changed are their first thought when "Spanish" comes up. Not me, who comes over to help their kids with math and is in contention for valedictorian. Not Greek-, French-, Russian-faced me.

At the bottom of the hill, where the road curves, I take a right and head down past the commercial district, where a few halfway decent restaurants and weird stores keep opening and closing—"Get Thee to a Sunnery," the tanning place, and "Yoga for You."

At the end of the stores, I hang a left into what little "affordable housing" there is in this town, a small apartment building with a tired-looking gray façade and a dead bush by the front door.

I lock up my bike in the little courtyard in the back and run up the three flights of stairs to our two-bedroom. I open the door. My mother never locks it. When you live a quarter of a mile away from houses with Hummers and Jaguars in the driveways, it's pretty logical to think your two-bedroom is not going to be the first place hit.

My mother is in the kitchen, looking all drained, as usual. Maybe once, like in the wedding picture in the hall, she was pretty, with bright pink cheeks and shiny, long, straight brown hair. But now she looks like a dishrag washed too many times with stuff that's other colors. As soon as I spot her, she makes me mad. I don't know why.

Slam! My little brother runs into me full speed, nearly knocking me down. I know it's coming, but he always catches me off guard. Although he's a skinny kid who eats only once in a while, he packs a lot of force.

"You're going to knock me down!"

"What took you so long?" he says, bear-hugging me.

"Joey, I wasn't gone that long."

"It's Ho-say," he says. He says "Jose" like a gringo. Mentally, I curse my parents for the ten-thousandth time for naming him Jose instead of Joseph. Or Connor. Or Duke. Or something else that would fit around here. When he was born, I gave them the "We're in America now" speech, but they didn't listen. Joey doesn't seem to mind.

"Anyway, Ho-say, what have you been doing while I was out?"

"Watch cartoons with me!"

"No, seriously." But I know resistance is futile. He always wins at getting me to watch *SpongeBob* with him, so I know I might as well just give in. "Okay, but just one episode."

"Two. The new one where Patrick and SpongeBob have a fight is coming. New episode!"

I follow him into our living room and sit on the couch. There are holes in the wicker on the sides of the couch, where first my little fingers and now his have poked through absently while watching TV. I spy a hole I created during one particularly long winter of watching *Johnny Bravo*. The cushions are a yucky pea-green soup color, worn through near where the back of your knees go.

He puts his hand in mine, and it gets sweaty in sixty seconds flat, but he is zombie-fied. He stays that way during the two episodes of *SpongeBob*—jaw slack, hand in mine, saying every three minutes or so, "That was funny, right?" He leans his head on my shoulder, as if doing that will convince me it was. It works. I laugh.

"I have a book I want to go read, little J man."

"But it's summer."

"School's about to start, and I want to finish the reading list."

"I thought you said you read all the ones you were supposed to read."

"I did, but I want to read the whole list."

"Why?"

"I just do."

"Okay," he says. "You read here with me and I'll watch cartoons."

The kid is going to make a hell of a negotiator someday.

I hear the front door slam and I tense up. He's early. Not good. Usually I can count on him coming home when it's time for me to go to sleep, so I can retreat to the room my brother and I share and stay out of his way. But now it's dinnertime and he's already here. So many things can go wrong in three hours. So many things usually do.

He walks into the living room, and you can almost see the cartoon dark squiggly lines over his head. He carries his mood around him like an angry cloud. I stare at the floor to avoid eye contact.

"So, you don't say hello to your father?"

"Hello," I mumble at the brown linoleum. Eye contact is bad. But not talking is bad, too.

Jose runs off the couch and wraps himself around our father's legs, creasing his black pants. "The robot, the robot! Let's play the robot!" Jose jumps up and down while still holding on.

My father takes off his red waiter's jacket, messes up Jose's gold, curly hair, and pries him off, saying, "In a little while," and walks a few steps to our kitchen/dining/everything room.

"What's for dinner?" my father asks.

My mother looks a little more wrung out than five minutes ago. "Lentils," she says.

"Lentils again?" he groans. I have to give it to him on this one. Damn lentils. Another meal brought to you courtesy of a ninety-nine-cent bag of beans. Maybe if I just don't eat until school starts I'll look skinny and I can wear those black jeans to our first dance. Lentils are the best motivation for a starvation diet when they are the only things in the house to eat.

CHAPTER THREE

On the first day of school, I breeze into homeroom, where my all-time favorite teacher, Ms. North, is *finally* my homeroom teacher. Geek alert: it's kind of a thing I've been looking forward to for years. I can't exactly explain it, but I want to be around Ms. North as much as possible, like she's got some secret code I need to crack. Bonus: she's also my first period class. So I don't have to navigate much of anywhere until well past 9:00 a.m.

As first period starts, Ms. North stands up. No one has been saying much of anything because her reputation precedes her.

"So, here you are. The few, the brave. The ones who signed up for two English classes in one school year. Your fellow students no doubt said you were crazy for doing it. And they are probably right, if sane means doing what's easy and what everyone else does. But I would like to think that is not what you are."

She starts passing out the syllabus. I start to hear soft groans— no one dares groan too loud. There is a book a week most weeks. I notice she's made what I hope is a joke next to Dante's *Inferno* ("extra points if you read it in the original Italian!"), and I see a bunch of books whose titles and authors I don't recognize—*Lucifer's Hammer*?—peppered in with a few of the old standards.

"Life, death, meaning, why we're here, whether society helps or absolutely corrodes the human experience, that's the topic of this class. If you just came for the college credits, ring out now." She points to the big brass bell hanging next to her blackboard.

A few people look around, but most everyone sits absolutely still. There are only us hard-core NHS girls in here, ten in total. And we've all had her before, so we know what we're in for.

"Okay, good. Don't say I didn't warn you."

⚬⚬⚬

THE WAY GORETTI CAME INTO MY LIFE WAS THIS:

Two months before I was supposed to start kindergarten, a giant screaming match broke out between the Parentals. I listened behind the wicker couch on the cold floor of the basement apartment that we lived in at the time. The dual screaming in itself was weird, since my father was by far the louder screamer, so my mother rarely tried to match him.

It went something like, "*No*, Jorge, we can't just keep her home! That's crazy! You're crazy!"

"*I'm* not crazy! *You're* crazy! You want us all to get deported?

Go, then! You go to the school! Tell them you have a kid with no papers that you want to enroll! I'll pack your suitcase and have it ready! Because *I'm* not going, do you understand me? They're *government* schools. They check your immigration status with the *government*. You want to get us deported? You can go by yourself!" screamed my father.

Because . . . yeah. We're illegal.

"But what is she going to do home all day? Someone is going to see her! Know that she's not in school when she's supposed to be!" countered my mother.

"We'll teach her ourselves! We won't let her go outside during school hours!"

"No, Jorge! No! I won't allow that! She needs friends! A normal life!"

"We're moving to Argentina soon anyway! Who cares? She'll have friends over there! She has better than friends! She has family!"

"We've been moving to Argentina for *five years now*! And nothing! What if it's another five years? Should she just rot in this basement until then?"

There was crying, and thumping, and something got thrown at some point. All I know is that the next day, when my father was at one of his two waitering jobs, my mother grabbed my hand and took me to a big office where it was very cold. My mother had put on a skirt and blouse. Outside the office, she leaned down and said something she said to me a lot.

"Now, Monserrat Thalia, when grown-ups talk, children listen. You don't say anything, do you understand?"

"Yes."

"And you don't repeat anything we ever talk about, ever. You know we could get into a lot of trouble for being illegals, right?"

I had no idea what we had done to be fugitives from the law, but I nodded. Quiet. Check.

Inside the office, after what seemed like a forever wait, we were taken further in to a room with a man behind the most giant desk I'd ever seen. It was dark brown and carved with figures—a big building, a woman with a blindfold on. I wondered if her arms got tired from holding up those plates on a string that way.

"How can I help you, ma'am?" He was bald and a little blond and his Spanish sounded really funny, like he was trying to pretend he was someone else or something, making up a silly accent. He said his words all wrong, almost like he had a cramp in his tongue.

"Your sign says you do immigration work."

"Yes, I do."

"Well, my husband and my daughter and I are illegals, and I want to know if there is anything to do to get our papers."

"Yes, that's the million-dollar question," he said, shaking his head slowly a little, his eyes down. He asked her a bunch of questions I didn't understand, about my father's work, entries, exits. Who our family was and where they lived. Big, grown-up words.

All I know is that after about ten minutes, my mother started to cry and the guy behind the giant desk started to look really uncomfortable.

"But how can that be?" she asked him. "How can there be nothing we can do?"

"The laws are not very helpful, I'm afraid. Even for people with special skills or family in the country, the rules are difficult and contradictory. Those are all the deportation cases I'm fighting right now," he said, pointing at a wall full of papers. "It's a losing battle. Until they fix the law, I'm afraid there's not much you can do."

"Thank you for your time," she said, wiping her nose with a tissue he handed her. She pushed a handful of bills at him, but he put his hand up and shook his head no. Maybe because they were snot-filled he didn't want them.

"Thank you for letting me practice my Spanish," he said, which seemed to me like a really weird thing to say to a crying woman. But as my mother had asked me to, I said nothing except "Thank you" when he handed me a lollipop.

Our next stop was to a square little building with a giant cross in front of it. I waited, coloring quietly at a small coffee table, while my mother sat inside with a lady in a weird hat and a long dress.

And it's been Goretti ever since, the unpublic school.

❧

SATURDAY MORNING, CHELSEA OFFERS TO COME PICK ME UP, but I want to bike and I like heading toward her much better than her heading toward me.

You can see Chelsea's house from far away, the highest part of a hill that makes it overlook the others like it's the oldest, biggest, baddest sibling on the block. I once heard Chelsea's mom call Willow Falls "the last great bastion against McMansions," supposedly because there are a lot of rules about what you can build and how it can look. Chelsea's mom and grandmother grew up in Willow Falls, and her dad grew up not too far from it. I've always wondered what it must feel like to have a sturdy string of history tethering you to a place, giving you the right to be there.

Chelsea's car is on the circular drive, a little crooked, next to her mother's hot red European two-seater, the car Chelsea calls "Mom's Midlife Mobile."

"Hi, Mrs. O'Hara," I say.

"M.T.," she says, smiling.

"How are you today?" I am the Parent Whisperer. Parents love me. I think the trick is actually talking to them, something their own kids usually don't do. If Mrs. O'Hara was my mom, I would talk to her all the time.

Mrs. O'Hara's kneeling down on a little foamy-looking thing, which matches her rubber boots, her gardening gloves, and the little garbage pail next to her, all an understated plaid. She's wearing a golf shirt with their country club's logo on it and khakis that I would have already gotten way muddy if I'd been putting stuff in the dirt.

"I'm good, I guess," she says, putting down her little digging thingy and raising her hand to the crown of her gardening hat, looking at me.

"I decided I'm going to plant an obscene amount of iris."

"How many?"

She points to some boxes I hadn't noticed behind her car. "Six hundred and fifty-seven."

"*Plants?*" I ask.

"Yep. Crazy, right? I had the gardener prepare the bed. But there is just something about putting them in the dirt that I want to do myself. I read the instructions on the Internet. I can do this." She looks down the driveway for a second. Then, "You know what I like about iris?" she asks.

"What?"

"You have to plant them in the fall. If you plant them earlier, they don't bloom. But you put them in the ground in the fall and then they get snowed on and they just look like dead little stumpy things for months, roots half exposed, and you're sure nothing good could ever come of them. Then the spring comes and they fan out and grow the most amazing flowers you've ever seen—seven, eight inches big, every color combination you can imagine—yellow, red, blues, orange, bicolors."

"Wow."

She stares off a little again. "I'm sure Chelsea has mentioned something about what happened here over the summer. But of course it goes without saying that I love Chelsea very much and that I'm glad she's got you."

"Ummm . . . yeah." I have no idea what she's talking about. Chelsea hasn't mentioned anything.

"I want you to know that I'm still the same person and my house is still always your house and that things are complicated, but they don't affect you and hopefully not Chelsea too much either."

"Yeah, of course." I don't know what else to say now. "Well, good luck with your six hundred and fifty-seven iris," I say, and smile.

"You have fun. Chelsea's inside."

I go in the house by the side door, the one everyone uses to avoid the palatial wooden double doors that weigh a ton and are carved with leaves and columns and hold giant matching iron door knockers. Up a curving staircase, down a hall, and to the right is Chelsea's room. I knock and don't wait for an answer before going inside.

"So . . . your mom was in the mood to chat this morning."

"Please, don't get me started on her. She's out there defacing the lawn."

"She said something about something that happened this summer? What's up with that?"

"Whatever. Anyway, far more important topic of discussion: Jonathan—to call or not to call?"

"Not to call."

"Yes, yes, I know the answer. It's a trick question to see if you're holding to our pact of forcibly restraining me if I even think about going back to him. On to other things. I already have reading to do for Monday. What about you? What does your schedule look like?"

"I have North first for Drama and Novel, then physics, Italian Four, calculus, English Four, American History . . ."

"Stop right there, you're giving me a headache. What the heck, Thalia-nator? We're supposed to hang out and have fun this year. We have devastatingly fabulous looks to orchestrate for prom and senior year boyfriends to catch and then discard. Do you really need

THE SECRET SIDE OF EMPTY

to take *two* North classes *plus* physics and calc?"

I want to say that this could be the last year I get a formal education. Instead I say, "Don't worry about me and these classes. We'll have plenty of fun."

I can pass most tests without a lot of effort. I sit in class when it's taught and then I just kind of know it for the test. I read fast. And I know what teachers want. I've signed up for a lot, but I can handle it.

"School's so easy for you. You're so lucky," she says.

I'm lucky, she thinks. I want to laugh but it would come across as mean. So all I say is, "Yeah."

"So what do you want to do?" asks Chelsea.

"Let's go into the city."

"Only if we can lie and say we're going to the library." She used to get along so well with her mother. I don't understand why she seems so angry with her recently, wanting to lie instead of just asking permission, which her mother would probably give.

"You choose your own cover stories. My mom won't even know," I say.

"Awesome. Let's go."

CHAPTER FOUR

New York City is about a half an hour away by train. Washington Square Park is a ten-minute subway ride from Penn Station. It's our favorite place to go. We sit on the grass, facing the arch, watching the people walk by, making up stories about them.

"Okay, you do that one," Chelsea says, pointing with her chin.

"The one with the blue hair?"

"Yeah."

"She's . . . she's a physics whiz."

"Ha!"

"But she tries to be real cool about it, you know? Like, doesn't get wrapped up in the geekiness of it. That's why the blue hair and the attitude. But she's really brilliant. But she's got a secret."

"You're so much better at this game than I am."

"You give me such good material," I say.

"So what's the secret?"

I look around, running my fingers over the grass, waiting for inspiration. "She . . . cheated on her SATs. So she feels like a fraud."

"But you said she was brilliant."

"Yeah, but deep down inside she doesn't believe it. So she paid someone to take the test for her. Now she feels terrible about it. Like everything she's accomplishing doesn't matter. It's eating her up inside."

The blue-haired woman with the plaid shirt tied around her waist makes her way through the park, past a juggler with a small crowd around him. She doesn't know she's just been a character in my game with Chelsea.

"I'm glad you suggested the city. It's definitely better than getting manicures, which is what I was going to suggest. We don't come here enough," says Chelsea.

"Yeah, it's pretty cool. Let's recap. We learned how to play singing bowls."

"Ate the best pizza in the history of pizza," breaks in Chelsea.

"Flirted with those NYU guys."

Chelsea looks around. The NYU Library is behind us. "We could come here, you know. NYU. Wouldn't it be fun to live right here? We could do this every day."

"I don't think this is what NYU students do every day."

"Where are you going to go? Have you thought about it? We have to start applying soon."

"Let me enjoy the last warm days of summerlike weather."

"But it might be nice to apply to some of the same schools. That way we can keep being, you know . . ."

"An awesome and formidable force?"

"Yeah."

"Her," I say.

"What?"

"It's your turn. You do her."

Chelsea looks over to where I'm pointing. Which means it works and I distract her.

"The freaky gypsy?"

"Yeah. Come on, she's an easy one."

We both look at her. She's got some flyers in her hand and a purple headband holding her unnaturally mahogany red hair squashed onto her head. She's wearing a cheap-looking belt of gold coins over her ripped jeans and a black lace shirt over a hot pink bra. She's of that indeterminate age, post-teenager but pre-too-old-for-everything-fun.

She catches us looking at her. We look away too fast. Too obvious.

"I think she's coming over here now," says Chelsea.

"She's handing out flyers."

She is, in fact, walking over to us. She walks down the path to us, and when she gets to the grass, she takes off her flip-flops to walk on it. It's weird that she's making a beeline for us, but I guess that's why we come here, for weird things that don't happen in Willow Falls, New Jersey.

"Hi," she says, like we've been waiting for her, like we had plans to meet.

"Hi," I say. Chelsea nods.

"I feel like you need a reading."

"A what?" I ask.

"A reading." She pulls out a tattered deck of oversized cards from a beaded bag with an elephant on it. A receipt flutters to the ground.

"Oh, you're like a tarot card reader?" asks Chelsea.

"Thanks, but we're all set," I say. "We'll take a flyer."

"No, I don't think you need a flyer. You need a reading," says the tarot woman. I am trying not to make eye contact, but I can feel her stare on my cheeks.

"I don't have any money, so . . . no thanks."

"Well, you do have money, because little suburban girls don't come into the city penniless. But it's not about money. I just get these feelings about people. Maybe something in the way you were looking at me."

"We were playing a game. People watching. I told my friend here to make up a story about you. Not in a bad way. It's just this thing we do."

"How about this? I give you a reading. If after it you feel you got something of value, you pay me whatever you think is fair. If you don't, you make up the story about me and we just had a nice chat. I'll even give you material. I was born in Kenya while my father was working there. My mother died giving birth to me. My father came home and bought an adobe house in the desert. I've had three lovers in my life, each of them missing something vital which I couldn't live without. There? See? I did half the work for you. So . . . a reading. What do you say?" She smiles, showing a full mouth of gorgeous, blindingly white teeth.

"We're not going anywhere," Chelsea says, a little nervously, like she's trying to figure out the woman's angle, whether she's some front for a white slavery ring or a drug dealer.

"Right here on the grass," says the woman, still smiling.

I look to Chelsea. "It'll be fun."

"You," says the tarot lady, waving her cards in my direction. "I like doing the skeptics."

"Okay," I say. Not sure how she knows I'm a skeptic, which I am.

She shuffles the cards with her eyes closed for a freakishly long time. I look around, wondering what we must look like to people passing by. Finally, she stops, pulls a shiny purple scarf out of the elephant bag, then spreads it carefully on the grass. She starts putting down cards.

"The Fool," she says. *Wait, is she calling me a . . .* "See this card here? It's called the Fool. You're starting a journey, leaving things behind, looking for what's next."

I try to keep my face blank so she won't read anything in it. I know people like her are good at getting clues from things like clothes and facial expressions. I want to give her as little as possible. I want to stump her.

"Lots of swords, the cards of intellect. You like school; you're good at it. You've got it figured out."

Chelsea blurts out, "M, you've got to admit that's amazing."

I want to shush her but I don't.

"You're all here," she says, pointing to my head.

She looks down at the cards. She's looking at one that's dark, with something that looks like the Leaning Tower of Pisa on it, except it's not leaning. It's surrounded by flames and badly drawn little people are either falling or jumping out of it.

"What's that?" I ask.

"Your obstacle. The Tower." She takes a deep breath in, like she's trying to figure out how to tell me something.

Despite wanting to stay cool, I say, "What is it?"

"Most people consider this a very negative card. But I think that's shortsighted. See how over here you got the Wheel of Life? Things come, things go. Life is like the wheel, going around and around."

"But what does the Tower mean?"

"Some people think it means disaster. But it just means a big change. It can feel like a disaster, but in the end, after it's over, it's what was supposed to happen."

"But what is it that's supposed to happen?"

"The cards don't work that way. They give you clues, but it's not like a detailed news report or anything. I just see a change."

"That feels convenient. It's not hard to predict that *something* will happen."

"Oh, little one who wants it all to make sense." She smiles, putting her hand on mine, although she can't be more than ten years older than I am. "Just remember that when someone tells you that things aren't going to end well, that's just because they want you to be afraid. Things always end well. Because they never end."

She puts down a few more cards.

"You are . . . starting school?"

"It's September and we've established I'm a little suburban girl, so . . ."

"Not college yet."

"Senior year," chimes in Chelsea.

"I see delays for you," she says, looking at me with her eyes, so dark they're even darker brown than mine. But hers are huge, not beady like mine.

"Delays?" I ask.

"Things not going the way you think they should."

"But you said it all works out in the end, right?"

"Is that what I said? Something like that."

Well, that stinks. Now I'm in a bad mood.

"Thank you very much," says Chelsea sweetly. The woman starts to pick up her cards and the purple scarf, but slowly. Chelsea pulls out a ten-dollar bill and hands it to her before I even realize the woman is waiting to get paid. Once she gets the ten, she walks away quickly.

I reach for my wallet, half to check if the tarot card woman was some kind of super-talented pickpocket. "Here, let me pay you."

Chelsea says, "I would tell you that was my back-to-school gift to you, but she was kind of a bummer. So let's just ignore her."

"All right, then I'll buy you an ice cream. Let's go." I pull Chelsea up off the grass. "And let's go back to play those singing bowls and find more NYU boys."

She gives me a little hug and smiles. She still smiles exactly like that first day in kindergarten. And she's still trying to make me feel good.

I HAD DREAMED ABOUT KINDERGARTEN FOR SO LONG, PACKING and unpacking and carefully repacking the little purple backpack my mother got me. But the reality of it had been nothing like what I'd expected. The first day, the teacher had introduced us to taking attendance.

"Okay, kids, I'm going to say your name and you have to sit very quietly. When I get to your name, you have to say, 'Here.'"

"Here!" screamed out about five or six kids.

"Wait until you hear your name, okay?"

"Janet?"

"Here!"

"Chelsea?"

"Here!" chirped the blond, tall girl sitting across from me.

"Quinn?"

The tiny redhead at my table shot up her arm and screamed, "HERE!"

"Sarah?"

Silence.

"Sarah?"

Someone elbowed a curly haired girl across the room and she stopped looking at the picture of the giraffe family and said, "Can I

THE SECRET SIDE OF EMPTY

go to the bathroom?"

"Are you Sarah?"

"Yes."

"Okay, we're getting to know each other, so just give me a minute, okay?"

"Okay."

"Munsee . . ." I saw the teacher start to struggle. Oh God. My name was next. Monserrat Thalia. The name no one on the playground could ever learn how to say. She started again. "Munsayratt? Munsayratt? Is that right?"

I sat there frozen, eyes wide. Maybe if I didn't say anything she'd never know it was me. But I guess the look on my face gave me away.

"Is that you, sweetheart? Am I saying that right?"

"Wait, hold on," said Quinn. "Her name is Mousy Rat?"

"Quinn, now, in this classroom we're kind to one another."

"I'm just asking what her name is."

"We also don't speak out of turn, please. You wait to be called on. Okay?"

I shivered a little, wondering if the teacher was going to keep trying to get my name right. But she moved on. And I decided I hated kindergarten.

Later that afternoon, Mrs. Yarrow made us color. I usually got the box of eight and colored with them carefully. But for kindergarten my mother had gone all out and bought the impossibly big box, with colors like chartreuse and cadet blue. And silver. My favorite. In the week before kindergarten started, I had worn down the silver crayon the most, always being careful to color around all its sides so as to not ruin its point. I had drawn a fish and a microscope and a magical little planet floating in space in a sea of deep blue, which really brought the silver out.

That day, while we colored, Quinn had zeroed in on my silver crayon and had snatched it out of my box without asking. My English was still spotty then. I'd learned most of it from commercials and TV shows. I wasn't sure I knew enough to ask Quinn to give it back. I tried to think of the words.

Suddenly, I heard the silver crayon snap in two. Quinn gave a little shrug and dropped it back on my desk.

I wanted to tell her she was a jerk. I wanted to tell her my mother had had to save up for those and I didn't know how long it would take until I would get another box. I wanted to tell her that crayon was good for making rocket ships and crowns on princesses and magic moon flowers and that she had ruined everything. But I couldn't.

So instead I burst into tears.

"What is it?" said Mrs. Yarrow.

I pointed to the broken crayon.

"Mousy Rat's stupid crayon just snapped. It was already broken. I don't know why she's making a big deal of it. It's just a crayon," said Quinn.

"Now, Quinn, let's be respectful of other people's things and also their feelings. Say sorry."

"Sorry," she said, narrowing her eyes and scrunching up her old-looking mouth. Looking about as unsorry as you can look while saying "Sorry."

Mrs. Yarrow turned to me, "And sweetheart, you're a big girl now, so stop crying. Use a different color. Look how many you have!"

I looked at the empty spot where the silver one should be and cried some more. I had spent an hour taking each crayon out and putting them back in rainbow order. Now there would always be a hole where the silver one should be. I cried harder.

Chelsea looked at me with her big Chelsea eyes. She waited for Mrs. Yarrow to walk away. Without saying anything, she took her silver crayon out of her box—her box was even bigger than mine—and slipped it in exactly the right empty spot in mine. Her thin fingers were graceful. She had chipped Granny Smith–green nail polish. I stopped crying and looked at her, then at the crayon. Her silver crayon was pristine, untouched. She smiled and looked down

at her paper, going on with her work. I sucked my boogers back
into my nose and went back to coloring mine, too.

It was then I knew I wanted to stick by this girl for life.

CHAPTER FIVE

My room is narrow, with Jose's little twin bed on one side and my folded-up futon on the other. It doesn't feel mine much, maybe because it's the fourth bedroom I've had in as many years. I bump my head into the model airplane hanging from a clear wire. I'm pretty sure that big chunk of dust has been on it since about three apartments ago.

We are what people would call poor. People around here, anyway. The trouble with having parents with no papers: they can't get very good jobs. You need a Social Security number for everything from garbage man to clerk at Walmart. So being an office dude with health insurance and paid vacation time is definitely out. There are some jobs that pay cash that look the other way if you don't have a Social Security number. I'm not sure how information about those jobs spreads, but somehow my dad hears about them.

In Argentina, my dad dreamed of being an architect. But no one in his family had gone to college, and he left school after his sophomore year in high school. At twenty-two, he came to America. He wanted to save up money and go back home to start a little business. He might not be able to be an architect, a professional, but he'd be a businessman.

But even when I was little, he still used to talk about architecture. He loved drawing and dreaming things up. He used to get architecture books and sketch late at night. I'd find his drawings scattered all over our little plastic table.

Now he is thirty-nine, and he is still a waiter. And he doesn't draw or make models anymore.

I sit on the futon and look at the model airplane for a second. It's got to be about six or seven years since we built that model together. The day we made it, it was raining outside. I remember because he came in out of the rain and his jet-black hair drooped a little over his forehead, but he was still handsome. He turned and half-handed, half-threw me the box under his arm.

"I found a Messerschmitt," he said.

I wasn't quite sure what that meant. My brother hadn't been born yet. I was still young enough to want to be the boy he'd never had.

"Let's build it," I said.

He moved some of my mother's sewing off the Formica table and spent a long time organizing all the parts, sending me for glue and paper towels and cotton swabs. Finally, he started building.

"Okay, hand me the propeller."

"Can I glue this one, please?"

"You want it to be perfect, right?"

"Yes."

"Well then, just let me do it."

"But I want to help."

"You're helping me by getting me the stuff."

"What kind of plane is this again?" I asked.

He pointed to the box. "A German Luftwaffe Messerschmitt twin engine. This is an old model. I got lucky at the craft store." His eyes lit up. "You know, when we move to Argentina, we're going to have one whole room in our big house just for all our models. That will be cool, right?"

I said nothing.

"You love Argentina, right? You can't wait to go back?"

"I don't really remember Argentina. It wouldn't be like going back."

"No, of course, silly, you were a baby when you came here."

"So how can I want to go back?"

"Because it's where I'll be. And your mother will be. It's where all your people are. It's where you're from. We're only here temporarily."

"How will I see Chelsea when we go to Argentina?"

"That doesn't really matter. You have cousins over there. Your real blood. You love your cousins, don't you?"

"Well, I . . ."

"Of course you do. Hand me the plastic part, the top of the cockpit." I did, and he picked it up carefully with my mother's tweezers while holding the little glue tube in the other hand. "You're going to have the best life in Argentina. We're going to be rich and build our round house. Remember the round house blueprints I showed you? With that big room? The secret staircase? Mendoza is the best place on earth. Not gross and humid like here, with all these bossy people."

"But I've only ever been here. This feels like home to me."

He looked away from the model and raised his eyes to meet mine and straightened his spine slowly. I felt his mood change, like a cold wind that gets in your mittens and up your coat.

"This isn't home. You're just a kid. You don't know what you're talking about."

"But what if . . . when I'm a grown-up . . . what if I wanted to stay here?"

"Now you're just being ridiculous."

"I'm just asking."

"Well, you can't, because we're going home. We're illegal here, so you can't stay anyway, even if we wanted to, which we don't. Now hand me the wheels."

A FEW DAYS LATER, MY MOTHER'S COUSIN CAROLINA IS SITTING at the kitchen table when I get home. Her baby, Julissa, is on the brown linoleum, picking at a little corner that is broken and peeling.

It makes me furious that Julissa is on the floor, eating linoleum. Who chooses who gets to be a linoleum eater and who gets to grow up on marble floors, like the ones at Chelsea's house? Julissa is a baby and she doesn't know that she got some life lottery ticket that won her broken brown linoleum instead of marble. She won't know for years, long after it's decided all kinds of important things in her life, like what kinds of school she'll get to go to and who she'll know.

I pick Julissa up. She smiles her four-tooth smile. I pick a little piece of linoleum off her bottom lip. For a second, I want to kick Carolina, not for losing sight of Julissa, but for bringing a baby into a brown-linoleum world at all.

"I swear she's bigger than last week," I say, trying to put the linoleum out of my mind.

"The way she eats! She eats everything! I make her garbanzos and she mostly mashes them all over her head, but she gets enough of them in her mouth that she's getting to be a fat little girl!"

Julissa gurgles and coos at her mother's voice. We all laugh.

"And you? Finishing school this year, huh?"

"Yes, I just started senior year."

"Your *abuela* back home must be so proud."

It hadn't occurred to me that my grandmother in Argentina would even know, or care.

"When I came here from Argentina a few years after your parents, you were a baby like Julissa. And your *abuela* waited every week for pictures to come in the mail, I remember. Imagine now that you're all grown up. And the first one in the family to graduate high school." She turns to my mom. "You have a good *suegra*; you're lucky. Too bad she is so far away."

"Yes, she was always good to me after I married her son. Although I do think maybe she thinks it's my fault that we stay here," says my mother.

"Ah, mothers with their firstborn boys. You know!"

"Yes, she babied him a lot. She combed his hair for him until he was thirteen!" laughs my mother.

"She'd probably *still* be combing it if he was still back home!" They both giggle.

Carolina turns to me. "So, do you think you'll go one day? To Argentina?"

"Well, there is the problem with the papers. I can't leave the U.S. Or I guess I could leave, but I won't be able to come back." It's okay to say this to Carolina because she's got the same issue.

"They can't keep up these stupid laws like this forever. They want us to work in their businesses, but they don't want to let us stay here legally, get licenses, have normal lives? It can't stay that way."

"Bah, politics, forget about it," says my mother.

"But, really, Monse," says Carolina to me. "If papers weren't an issue and you could come and go as you pleased, would you ever go live back home?"

"This *is* home."

"That's how it is," she says to my mother, raising her hands in the "I don't know" position, as if I'm not here. "The kids grow up here and they don't know anything else. It's natural."

"Not everyone understands that," says my mother quietly.

"That's why we've got to save up and get Julissa home before she's old enough to think like that. Paco talks about it all the time. But it's so hard to save. And go back there for what? No jobs. The crime rate . . . it's a shame what's happening in our country."

"There are no good answers," says my mother, putting the maté gourd with the little chopped up green leaves and the spoonful of sugar inside in front of Carolina, then filling it up with boiling water from her thermos.

Julissa grabs a piece of my hair and tries to put it in her mouth. I make a face at her and she giggles. She is so little and oblivious.

Her fate is entirely outside her own hands. Maybe Carolina and Paco will go, and maybe they will stay here without papers. Either way, Julissa will be living out the consequences of those decisions for the rest of her life.

Suddenly Jose slams into me from behind. "*SpongeBob* is starting! Come on!" And I'm relieved to just stare at a little yellow sponge for a while.

❦

GROWING UP IN WILLOW FALLS, I ALWAYS SAW THAT OTHER people had more than I had. But for the longest time it was just a thing that was, like the sky being blue or how old teachers always seem to have mustaches. It wasn't until the end of sophomore year that it occurred to me that I could do something about my financial situation.

One day at lunch, Patricia from geometry had come over with some formula she just couldn't get, and I'd explained it to her on a napkin.

Patricia said, "Wow, that's awesome. Why can't Prune-strand explain it like that? Thanks."

Chelsea, looking up as Patricia walked away, said, "You should charge for that."

It started slowly. But by the start of junior year it was known I was for hire. Patricia's little sister was one of the first ones I started tutoring. Then came her friend and that little freshman who lived on Chelsea's block and always mumbled through her stringy brown hair. I specialized in math—the most tutorable subject—but also critiqued and edited English papers and social studies projects. I found out what a local teacher was charging for the tutoring he was doing on the side and underbid him by twenty dollars an hour. It was still more cash than I had ever seen.

Business is still strong. Of course, no seniors want tutoring—they will be getting into college with their junior year grades, so they're looking to coast. But I have my old-time customers, plus a whole new crop of clueless, baby-faced freshmen to tutor. Sometimes I think they just like an excuse to come up and talk to a senior, saying things like, "You're still coming to my house this afternoon, right?" But everyone knows it's a business thing, so it doesn't do anything bad for my reputation.

By now, I have $175 saved up. I keep every crisp and wonderful bill in the inside pocket of my journal. At this pace, I may be able to buy myself an inexpensive laptop before Christmas. I'll buy my brother a DVD player and a bunch of seasons of *SpongeBob*. I'll make sure I have enough clients so I can hook up Wi-Fi and pay for it every month and maybe even buy a prepaid cell phone.

I walk in from school and into the kitchen. My father is

waiting for me at the table. It takes me a minute to figure out what he's holding in his hands: my spiral-bound journal, open to the middle, exposing my beautiful little stash of earnings.

"What the hell is this?" he asks me, his eyes open scary-wide. I should have known that my "I Have Money" Happiness Train would screech to a halt in You Didn't Ask Your Father Station.

"Money." Note to self: Hide journal better.

"Don't be smart with me. Where did you get it?"

"Tutoring." I mean, does he want me to be stupid with him?

He snaps his head toward my mother, who is looking grayer than usual. He says to her, "And did you know about this?"

"Well, she said she wanted to help some kids and she needs a computer and—"

He snaps back toward me, a vein popping out of his forehead now. "So you're begging your friends for money now? Don't you have any pride?"

"I'm not begging anyone for—" His smack stops me in mid-sentence. Being hit makes me furious. The bone in my face screams out from the impact.

I stay very still, because I have long learned not to give him the satisfaction of reaction or movement. The furious feeling makes its way down my face, to the back of my neck, to my stomach. I bore a hole into the floor with my heat vision and channel all my energy into fantasizing about doing bad things to the hand he smacks me with.

He starts screaming. You never know what's going to set him off, but you sure know where he's going once he gets started. He points to my mother. "You! I blame you! She's seventeen years old! What the hell does she need to be working for! Won't she have enough years of misery ahead of her? Enough years to be a slave? Is that what you want for her? To be a slave, always taking orders from people?"

"Me or you?" I say.

This makes him livid, and he smacks me again, harder, then again. *Good.* I want to make him livid. It's the one thing I can do.

"You think you're so smart! You think a computer is going to make a difference for you! But who are you? You are nothing! You can't do anything in this country. You hate Argentina so much, but Argentina is your only chance, because in this country you're dirt, you're nothing! Serving these losers who think they're better than you. Do you hear me?"

The Inuit can hear him.

"You need a computer? For what? You can't get a real job here. You can't go to college. Stop fooling yourself! And if you ever sneak around behind my back like that again, you are going to be very sorry."

He reaches into my journal pocket, takes the $175, and slips it in his pocket.

"No little smart-ass is going to keep her own money while she's living under my roof!" He throws my journal at me, and the things I kept in the little pocket in the middle flutter to the floor: a pressed flower I picked on a walk with Chelsea and a folded copy of Shakespeare's Sonnet 116, which blew my mind the first time I read it so I made a photocopy of it at the library.

I know my money is going toward rent or some other household expense. I'll never see it again. But I make two vows. One, I'm going to steal my money back out of his pocket from his tip money one dollar at a time if I have to.

And two, I am going to find a better hiding spot for the money I make from now on. I will sabotage and I will carry out stealth actions. When you don't have armies, you go to guerrilla warfare.

CHAPTER SIX

am in a supernova fury when my mother walks into my room. I feel the overwhelming urge to throw something at her. In this moment, I hate her more than I hate him. Something about letting all of this happen, and then walking in here wrapped in a cloud of her own powerlessness as her excuse.

"How's your face?"

I just stare past her, at a spot on the wall where I wrote "Stupid" in pencil about six months ago, which no one seems to have discovered.

"Monse, you just have to learn how to keep quiet."

This finally makes me look at her. "You're kidding, right?"

"You disrespect him. He just wants to get respect somewhere."

I point to my face, where he smacked me. "So this is okay?"

"No, of course it's not okay. I'm just trying to help you avoid that."

"So it's *my* fault?"

"It's not your fault."

"But I should keep quiet."

"It's just . . . you remember how he used to be?"

"He was always a jerk." Something feels vaguely off about this statement, like the things you say when you're trying to win an argument. For some ridiculous reason, I feel my eyes well up with tears.

She looks behind her nervously and lowers her voice as if someone's coming. "Remember how it was always him and you against me? And I was the wet blanket? And you with your long talks and playing Frisbee on Sundays and watching movies late into the night, always laughing together? Remember? Speaking English so I couldn't understand?"

"Oh, because I was an idiot when I was, like, four years old makes it okay that he hits me."

"That's not what I'm saying. I'm saying it's hard for him, too. You should see that."

"I don't need to see anything. I need to get the hell away from him is what I need."

"Don't say that."

"I'm saying that."

"Put yourself in his position. He came here a young man with a big dream. And look at where he is now."

"I don't care where he is now. Arrested is where he should be now, for hitting me. I wish you'd just leave me alone," I tell her.

And to my surprise, she does. She walks out of my room like she's a hundred years old. I fight the urge to throw a pair of balled-up socks at the back of her head.

I get on my bike and go to the library. I have nothing to do, no paper to type or anything due for school. I google "immigration laws" and "immigration amnesty" like I have so many times before. As usual, there is nothing. Nothing good, anyway.

SUBURBANITES SURE DO LOVE THEIR AMBIGENDROUS NAMES. The next day, I go tutor Mackenzie, who is a girl, and Cody, who is a boy. Mackenzie is Patricia's little sister. She can barely add but is some kind of lacrosse star who really needs to pass freshman math. Cody lives two doors down and heard about me from Mackenzie, whom he seems to be crushing on desperately.

In the middle of Mack's session, Cody walks in, trailed by the maid who let him in.

"Oh, are you guys still working? I thought you were coming over my house at four-thirty," Cody says. This is the third week he's done this.

"No, we said five o'clock, remember?" I point out, annoyed.

"It's okay," says Mackenzie. "We were just about done anyway."

We weren't, but the lesson is now officially over. Cody says something inane and Mack giggles and doodles spirals on the edges of her notebook. I still have to explain simplifying algebraic equations to her, but I've lost her. If she messes up on her math test, her parents might start to think that tutoring is not paying off and call in the big guns. Stupid Cody.

"Focus, Mack. Let's just get through the simplification process before we stop."

Mackenzie rolls her eyes. "I mean, seriously, am I ever going to need this in real life?"

"Mackenzie, passing math *is* real life. C'mon, look here. Can you simplify this problem further?"

Mack plays it off like she's going to try, but Cody is throwing little bits of rolled-up paper at her head. I look up and try to keep my patience. In the kitchen, which I can see from the family room because Mack and Patricia's house is what they call "open concept," Mackenzie's parents' housekeeper is slowly shining a granite countertop that is already so spotless it's blinding. It blows my mind that she is actually wearing a maid uniform. Did Mackenzie's parents buy it or does the maid wear it for kicks, being all retro about it?

Mackenzie sees me looking over at the kitchen and mistakes the look for interest in food.

"Yeah, I'm hungry, too," she says. "Marta, we need a snack."

Marta looks up and blinks a little, clearly confused.

"Hell-o. Anybody there?" She waves her hand in a slow and exaggerated way. "Marta, snack-o?" Mackenzie rolls her eyes. "Ugh. This one is new. Margarita, who I loved, just moved back to Guatemala, who knows why. Why would anybody go back there? This one's English is nonexistent."

"Please bring-o el snack-o." Mackenzie's having fun with this now, miming. My guts twist a little and I'm suddenly not hungry at all.

"No, it's okay, Mackenzie, we're fine. I should get over to Cody's."

"No, it's not okay that she won't get me a snack when I need one."

Marta is coming over, misunderstanding what Mackenzie is saying.

Not wanting to see this go any further, I blurt out, "*Ella dice que si nos puede traer algo de comer.*"

"*Ah, sí, algo de comer. Como guste,*" she says. *As you wish.* She turns toward the pantry full of bags and boxes of every imaginable processed food on the planet.

"M.T., you've really been paying attention in Spanish class, huh? I should get my parents to pay you to come over every day after school and translate for the maid."

All of a sudden my eyeballs are pounding. "Okay, so, look, I'm going to Cody's now, but you should work on problems eight through twenty-two. And watch nineteen, it's got that twist we were talking about before. Remember." I'm slamming books and getting my stuff ready.

Marta puts down a bowl of popcorn and a plate full of Fruit Roll-Ups on the table in front of us.

She turns to me and says, "*Gracias, mi hijita, pero es que yo no hablo mucho inglés todavía. ¿Y tú de dónde eres?*" Where am I from, she wants to know. I don't look like her kind to her. To her I look like Mackenzie and Cody's kind. But that's not what I am either.

I ignore her, my face burning. I know I'm being rude, but suddenly I have to get out of here. I heave my four-ton backpack on my back. "Cody, we've got to go."

Mackenzie slips me an envelope. On the upper left-hand corner it says, "Phillips, O'Connor and Jones, P.C., Attorneys at Law," with an address on Park Avenue in the city. Jones is her mom. Her dad owns some kind of business. I've never actually seen either of them. I take the cash out of the envelope on the way out, crumple the envelope up, and throw it in their recycling bin.

MACKENZIE'S AND CODY'S MONEY FEELS HEAVY IN MY POCKET. I don't want to go home. My dad is working a dinner shift, which means he won't be home until after 11:00. I told my mom I'd be at Chelsea's until 6:00, which is now, but I don't have any way to call her and let her know I'll be late since our phone got cut off a week ago for nonpayment.

After Mackenzie's and Cody's spotless granite caverns, the thought of being in my apartment makes me almost vibrate with energy I can't keep inside.

I pound on my bike pedals, past lawns and hills, water fountains, columns, the freaking Coliseum, Japanese sculptures, a picture-perfect wooden fort. It's too early for most of them to be home from the city, where they all work, the owners of these homes. Their enormous homes all sit empty, except for the Martas polishing them, waiting for the owners' return.

I pedal harder.

Finally, a right turn and a left and I'm on the strip, on the Ann Taylor side. I prop my bike up against a streetlight made to look like an old-time gaslight. I don't have a lock since I usually only bike to people's houses.

That's what I'll get, a bike lock. I know I want to save for a computer, but suddenly the thought of spending my sixty dollars feels amazing, like I'm a little lighter. A better me.

I walk into the pharmacy superstore and get a basket. There aren't many bike lock options, but the more expensive one looks better, sturdier, so I throw that one in the basket. Next I head over to the makeup aisle. I'm not much of a makeup wearer, but maybe I need to change that. I hover around the eye shadow. They're like paints in art class—dark, light, shiny, flat. I want them all. I settle on a shiny forest green and a sparkly beige for my eyelids. Maybe if I put on green eye shadow, my eyes will look greener. Anything would be better than my dark, small, ugly brown eyes.

And next a journal. After seeing mine in my father's hands, all of a sudden I can't touch it anymore. I need a new one. And not some dollar-store spiral notebook, but a real journal. Maybe even leather bound.

I wander over to that section and see what they have. Baby's first year. Inspirational quotes. Gag. As I'm combing over the five options, I hear behind me, "Hey?"

I look up. It's Soda Guy from the other night. He's not quite as tall as I remember him. But his eyes are lighter. He's in jeans and a sweatshirt.

I guess I stare too long, because he shifts his weight a little from his left leg to his right. "I'm from the other night . . . remember? The car, the dead end?"

"Yeah, yeah, I remember. You were in Brian Ferriss's car."

"Yeah, hi, I'm Nate," he says.

"Hi, Nate." I really want to say something else, but nothing is coming to mind.

"You're Sean's sister's friend, right? So . . . what's your name?"

"Oh, yeah, I'm M.T." I brace for the joke. EMT? Mother Trucker? He spares me.

"M.T., nice to officially meet you." He does air quotes around "officially." He is cute when he does air quotes.

"So that was weird the other day, right?" he says.

"Awkward and weird, yeah." Boy, I am scoring points for sparkling conversation.

"Awkweird." He smiles. I laugh. He looks pleased.

Then I look down at the journals.

"Yeah, so, you're busy, I just saw you and . . ."

I really don't want him to go, so I scramble around for a reason to keep talking. I hold up two journals, one yellow with buttercups on it, one with bluebirds in orange boxes, facing in all directions.

"Which one?"

He scrunches up his nose. "Hmmm . . . of those two?"

"I know. Options are slim."

"Yellow flowers for sure."

I laugh, put the bird journal down, and hug the buttercup one to my chest. "Yellow flowers it is."

As he walks me over to the register, he says, "So you don't go to Willow. We've established this."

"No, I go to the girls' school."

"Oh, you're one of the Goretti Goddesses? Is it true the nuns beat you guys with rulers?"

"Not if they know what's good for them. We hit back."

He laughs and bumps into me for no good reason, like he wants to get into a wrestling match. I wonder briefly if I could take him. That thought is followed by amazement that this super-cute guy is hanging around looking clumsy, doing a whole lot of staring at his feet.

After I pay, we stand, all "where do I put my arms." Someone goes by and the alarm goes off. The bored clerk waves them on without looking up. I wish for a split second that I had the guts to stuff my pockets full of eyeshadow and walk out past the detectors, all calm and cool.

Over the noise of the alarm, Nate says, "So, Willow's having a dance on Friday. You should go."

"Oh, I think my friend Chelsea said something about going." It is a total lie, but he doesn't know that.

"So maybe I'll see you there."

"Yeah, maybe."

I toss the bag, receipt, and packaging to all my new things in the trash can outside, then stuff them all deep in my backpack. I like the idea of erasing evidence. It feels like a superpower.

CHAPTER SEVEN

"A Willow dance, are you serious?"

"C'mon, Chels, just this one time."

"But their dances are so lame."

It's true. Willow Falls Regional High School dances *are* lame. Maybe something about their monstrously big gym that never looks full, or the DJs they get, or the way that everyone hangs out in little pockets by cliques. The all-black clad crowd—they must be the theater geeks or the art crowd—stand outside the actual gym, looking too bored to be there. The cheerleaders, who I know by sight from town football games and general cheerleaderiness, wear clothes that are too tight, topped off by too-perfect blond hair. There is always a cluster of the Antisocial Pot Smokers type there, smelling of pot. I wonder why they come at all.

"I really want to see him," I tell Chelsea. Of course I have told her every moment of the Encounter at the Pharmacy in microscopic detail, nanosecond by nanosecond, and we have deconstructed the code locked inside his words for an hour already. I know if we are on a boy mission there is no question she will come to the Willow dance with me.

"I'll go if you do something for me," she says.

"Sure, what?"

"Come with me to Siobhan's school next weekend."

"Oh come on, Chelsea."

"Why not?"

"I just—there's that paper, and I have a calculus test the Monday right after that and . . ."

"Siobhan's not that bad, you know. You can study in the car on the way back. And it's not like you're going to study for it anyway and you know that. Please come."

I am surprised that Chelsea has picked up on me not liking Siobhan.

I really want to do what Chelsea wants. But the thought of going to see the whole college experience unfold right in front of me, like a sick little buffet of desserts in front of a homeless, hungry person, makes me want to crawl under my covers and not come out until nothing matters anymore, like when I'm twenty-four. Plus there's Siobhan. Make that twenty-five.

"I'll ask my mom, but you know how my Parentals are," I say. They can always be counted on to mess things up.

"I'll come ask with you." Uh-oh, Chelsea means business.

"No, no, I'll ask, I mean it." The thought of Chelsea in my

apartment makes me queasy. It's an unspoken thing between us that since she's clearly got the better crib, we always go to her place instead. Chelsea in my apartment feels like the princess at the city dump. It's just not done. I'd better ask with enthusiasm or Chelsea will park herself on my mother's sewing machine and try to convince my father herself.

Chelsea drives me home.

I walk upstairs slowly, trying to figure out a way to do what Chelsea wants but also not go visit Siobhan. I push open the door to the apartment. The smell hits me right away.

Not freaking again. I can't believe it.

I make my way to the kitchen by touch only in the pitch black. There, Jose colors by the light given off by the kerosene camping lantern. My mother has put a few candles on the stove burners as well. They give the room a gloomy glow. She's wiping the middle of the stove in slow motion.

"So he didn't pay it again," I say.

"Business is slow at the restaurant," she answers slowly. She moves like her elbows and her shoulders hurt.

"I'm sure it is. How long is it going to be this time?"

"I don't know. I've asked to borrow money from a few people."

"Yeah, awesome."

"Did you want a candle to take with you to your room?" For

once my mother doesn't try to pretend like everything is okay. I guess she's not in the mood for me, either.

"I needed to ask you about something."

"What?"

"Two things, actually. One, there is a dance I want to go to on Friday."

"Yes, of course. Dances are fun. Did I ever tell you about the dance where your father and I met?" Dances are always good for an easy yes with her. I feel like I should listen to the story even though I've heard it before.

"I guess."

She lights up. "I was wearing a light blue dress my mother had made me. It had these little capped sleeves. It was a few days after my seventeenth birthday. Like the age you are now. My mother had made it for my birthday. I had on my one pair of good heels. I was so worried they'd get ruined because the road to the town square was all dirt and there were pebbles."

"So you tried to walk on tippy toes."

"And close to the *acequia* because the ground was less rocky there, yes. I wore my hair short then. My mother hated that. 'How are you ever going to catch a husband with your hair short like that?' she used to say." Her eyes have a faraway glaze and are all aglow with the kerosene lamp. It's like she's telling me the story of some fairyland she visited in her dreams a long time ago.

"I was getting to be an old maid. I know it sounds crazy, but that's how it was there. All of my friends had been dating the men who would be their husbands for a few years by then. My sister had been married maybe two years. She went to the dance, but she sat with the married women and didn't dance.

"I didn't want to get married. I thought I'd be a lawyer and help poor people. But by then I had been working and had stopped going to school . . . I don't know how long. A year, maybe?"

She looks at me like I know the answer. I want to squirm away, but know I need to sit here and listen to her.

"Anyway, when I got there I spotted him right away. I had never seen him before. I was so bored with all the boys from my town, but he was new. I found out later he had come from across the city with his cousin. He was so handsome! You've seen the pictures, right?"

Gag. There's the one up in the hallway. The two of them looking like clueless babies, all happy about God knows what.

"Yeah."

"He says he spotted me right away, too. And he was so bold, you know? I liked that about him. Other boys sort of stood around looking stupid, but he walked right up to me. My mother hated that about him! He was too fresh, she always used to say. But he asked me to dance and I did. And we danced together all night. At the end of the night, he walked me over to the little stand and bought me a soda, which was a pretty dashing thing to do. The boys from my town never spent money on us like that."

I stare at the candle on the stove. Hoping it will hypnotize me away from listening to this story again.

"So we took our soda and walked over to a little clearing. My mother was furious with me afterward for walking off with a strange boy like that! But we just sat and talked . . . it felt like forever. And do you know what he said to me?"

Of course I know. I've heard this story a hundred times.

But the proper response is, "What did he say?" So that's what I say.

"He said, 'I'm going to America and I'm going to be a very important man one day. How would you like to be a very rich man's wife?'"

"Ummm, Ma, you don't think that was a little weird?"

"Weird? No! It was romantic."

"But he'd just met you."

"I don't know. They were different times. A different place. People got serious fast over there. Not like here where there is all this dating and living together. We didn't do that there."

Still creepy.

"Anyway, so I had to act offended by that, of course. I couldn't act like a girl who thought it was okay to get propositioned like that by a stranger."

"You just said it was romantic."

She waves her hand in frustration. "Anyway, so what I said was, 'I just turned seventeen. I am a liberated woman. I'm not marrying anyone anytime soon. I'm going to have my own career.' And he said, 'When is your birthday?'"

"Wait, he just skipped over the whole career conversation?"

She gives me an irritated look. "I said, 'My birthday was three days ago.' And he got down on one knee." She is looking giddy. "He said, 'I am a poor man now and I didn't know I would meet the woman of my dreams here tonight. Let me give you the only thing I can give you tonight.' And so you know what he did?"

I do know, but I let her say it.

"He sang me a song. A love song. And when he was finished, he said, 'That was my first gift to you, but it won't be my last. One day I'll have whole orchestras for you on your birthday, and dresses and jewels. Anything you want.' And then he kissed me."

I want to say, "So how did that orchestra and jewels thing work out for you?" but that's mean even for me. So instead I say, "And making out the first time you met a guy was okay back then?"

"We did not *make out*. It was all very proper. We were married six months later." She's done. Thank God. "What was the other thing you wanted to ask me?"

"The other thing is that Chelsea wants me to go with her to some college visit thing she's doing. I told her it was stupid."

"I think that's a great idea," she says, like she's talking to the kerosene lamp. She's back to looking tired.

"It's, like, you know, a whole weekend. Leaving Thursday after school and getting home Sunday. I know it's so long."

"Yes, but it will be good for you to see a college from the inside."

"What's the point?" I ask her. She makes me so mad sometimes. Especially after that gross the-day-I-met-your-father story.

"You never know," she says.

She's ridiculous. I can't believe I'm going to have to convince her to say no to me.

"There are going to be parties and things like that," I tell her. "With boys. Maybe beer."

"I think you're a smart girl and you'll be responsible. Can you go to see a class, too?"

"I doubt it. I mean, it's not really that kind of weekend."

"That Chelsea is a good girl. I think it's a great idea. Don't worry about your father. Let me talk to him."

I can tell she's already made up her mind. My mother actually looks excited about it. I consider telling Chelsea that my mother said no and then hiding in the library for the weekend. Or maybe a Walmart, like the pregnant girl in that movie. I could move into Walmart, except I'm not sure where there's a Walmart around here. Maybe Saks at the mall. I could live just in that bathroom comfortably for a weekend. It's bigger than our apartment and it's got a whole lot less linoleum and lentils.

CHAPTER EIGHT

inally, it's Dance Day. Chelsea and I get to Willow Falls Regional fashionably late and walk the three miles between the parking lot and the gym. Okay, maybe not three, but a lot. Since Goretti is basically an overgrown house for a school, this place is kind of scary. Even if Nate is here, I probably will never find him with the gazillions of other people clogging up the walkways.

"Do you think we'll be able to find Laurie and them?" I ask, scanning the crowd for a familiar face. We know Laurie and a few of her friends from town soccer and, supposedly, it's on their invitation that we're here.

"Yeah, they said we'd meet by the vending machines outside the gym. But we shouldn't move in too big a pack or you'll look too intimidating for him to come up to you," says Chelsea. I wonder where she got the Boy Decoder Ring and if she'll let me borrow it.

Chelsea has had three Serious Boyfriends, including the last one, the unfortunate Jonathan. I've been sworn to keep her from him even if she goes temporarily insane and latches on to his leg as he tries to get away.

I have had none. I had my first kiss in the eighth grade with creepy little Matthew Gibbons. Plus that weird email thing with the kid from chemistry last year who used to write me all these sappy things but then never actually wanted to see me in person. I've had my share of "my friend says his friend says he says you might be cute"s along the way, but nothing that has ever turned into anything.

Laurie and her friends aren't by the vending machines. I take in a deep breath when Chelsea says, "Let's see if they're inside," and we step in the yawning jaws of their gym.

It's even bigger than I remember. If that's even possible. Giant banners line the top of walls: WILLOW FALLS REGIONAL, HOME OF THE RAIDERS. STATE CHAMPIONS. REGIONAL CHAMPIONS. Lacrosse, football, baseball. I guess if you've got, like, 200,000 students, a few of them must be good at everything.

The music bounces off the walls, tinny and uninspiring radio songs. Unless these guys have stadium-quality sound, there's no way they're going to get the volume high enough to matter. Everyone is in pockets, like I remember them, except for one group of surfer haircut guys who are dancing like maniacs right at the entrance, either hopelessly in need of attention or completely high. The freshmen look about four years old, hovering near the door, intimidated.

Finally, Chelsea spots them.

"Hey," says Laurie, "you made it."

"Yeah," says Chelsea.

"I don't know why we come to these. They're so lame."

"Habit?" I say.

"I guess. Plus it's weird that there will only be a few more of these and then we're all off to college."

Well, some of us. Isn't *somebody* going to slack in this crowd?

"You all right after practice?" says Joon, one of our best forwards, to Chelsea. Chels had an epic crash with someone's elbow during our last practice that looked like it might have rattled one of her eyeballs loose. I tried to get her to sit out for the rest of the practice but she wouldn't.

"Yeah, fine."

"I can't wait for college guys," says Laurie. "Everyone here is so useless."

I don't want to break it to her that it's these high school guys and guys just like these who will be college guys next year.

"No one interesting?" asks Chelsea. Good, Chelsea, good. I have instructed her to get whatever intel she can on Nate, but not to reveal my interest. "What about those tennis guys? We had the weirdest thing with them on the strip the other day."

"Who?"

"Ferriss. And some kid Nate. A few others."

"Oh, probably Jackson was there. Crazy, kind of hyper?"

"Curly black hair?"

"Yep, him."

"Yeah, he totally terrorized my cousin while she was visiting."

"He's nuts. The other ones are marginally normal. Ferriss has been going out with Tracy for, like, two years. Nate was seeing that girl from chem, what was her name?"

"Naomi," offers Joon helpfully.

Argh. Kick to the stomach.

"I thought they broke up?" says Laurie.

"I don't know. I thought someone said they saw them at the movies."

"No, they broke up at the end of the summer," says Laurie. "Anyway, he's cute, right?"

I shrug. I don't know these girls well enough to trust them with my hots for Nate. Plus, Nate and I had, like, one conversation. I don't want to seem all stalker-y and pathetic. Which I am, but he doesn't need to know.

The dance goes on like this, no sign of Nate, no dancing, just gossip and soccer talk, college visit stories. The Nate question is forgotten after three spectacular break-up stories, one involving an overdose of aspirin and a guy pulled out of school for a month of rehab. By the end of the dance, I'm tired of hoping. I'm feeling kind of stupid for making Chelesa suffer through a Willow dance for nothing.

"C'mon, Chels, we've got to get home."

"You sure you guys don't want to go to the diner?" asks Laurie.

"No," says Chelsea, "we should get home." I am sleeping over at Chelsea's house, and her parents are pretty strict on curfew.

We pull into Chelsea's drive, say a quick hello to her dad, who is watching a Vietnam documentary on what can only be described as a movie theater screen. We go up to her room. I change into sweats and a T-shirt, and Chelsea puts on pink pajama bottoms with hot pink monkeys on it and an old T-shirt from Boston College. She pulls her laptop on her lap while she chews on a Twizzler.

"So he didn't go," she says.

"I know, whatever."

She stares at her screen, then gets in closer.

"M, check it out. Laurie just posted a picture on her wall. Isn't that him?"

I scoot in next to her and look. Yes, it's him in a red sweater, crammed into a booth with Laurie, Joon, and a few other guys, all grinning wide for the camera. God, he looks good in red.

"Isn't that the diner? Laurie just posted it from her phone."

"Whatever."

"You should friend him," she says.

"I'm not friending him."

"I'm logging out and you're friending him."

"No, Chels! That's desperate. I don't want to."

"Fine, okay." She drops it, and I'm grateful. "But check your account if you want. I'm going to go brush my teeth."

As she pads off down the hall, I log into Facebook. The friend request icon is lit up with a red 1. I click on it.

Friend request from Nate Robinson. With an email. It says:

"Hey, Laurie said you were at the dance but I looked and looked and didn't see you. I got there kind of late, I guess that's why. I can't keep chasing you around town, so how about we be friends on here?"

I lift my hopes back up and hold them in my hands as I click "Accept."

THE KITCHEN IN CHELSEA'S HOUSE IS BLINDINGLY, SPARKLY white. There is a slab of marble on a giant island holding a bowl of apples big enough to stock the produce section of any reasonably sized supermarket. No one family could ever eat that many. Food as decor.

Chelsea grabs some frozen waffles and puts them in a toaster oven which is magically hidden behind some cabinet doors, like the refrigerator and everything else.

"So . . ." You can tell she's been holding the conversation off until the right time. "We're going to Siobhan's, right?"

"Yeah." I'm still a little stunned my parents agreed. But they did.

"So here's what I think we should do today. How about we go to the DMV so you can take your written test? We can practice driving all weekend and see if they'll take you for a driving test before we go on the road trip. We should have two drivers, just in case."

I can't get a driver's license, but I can't explain why to Chelsea. I've looked at the list of "points" you need even to apply to take the test. I don't have any of them. Social Security card. Passport. Birth certificate. I take a moment to throw little hate daggers in the general direction of my parents. For the thousandth time.

As we all started turning sixteen and a half, everyone began to take their driver's test. When my turn came, I blew it off with lame excuses. Chelsea was relentless for a while, but then she got old enough for her license and got her Beemer as a reward. She had dropped it. Until now.

"There's no way I can take the test before next weekend," I say.

"You never know. Let's go and ask."

"I haven't studied for the test."

"Oh, please, M, you helped me study so much you probably have that book memorized."

"Yeah, yellow means speed up, right?"

"I'll drive you by your place and you can get your birth certificate."

Why is Chelsea being a pitbull all of a sudden? My heart is pounding so hard I am afraid I might pass out.

"I don't think my mom keeps it there. I . . ."

"You wanna call her? We can drive her to the bank deposit box if she doesn't keep it at home."

Bank deposit box. That's funny. She's both my best friend and also someone who lives on a completely different planet. It's like she's a native and I'm trying to explain where I come from to her, but she's got no words for "road" or "building."

"Chels, seriously, I just don't want to."

"I don't get it. You can practice in my car."

She looks at me for a minute, then goes further than she's gone before. "M, you act like it's this big difference, that because my parents have more money than yours do it's, like, a thing."

"An ironic conversation to be starting over a slab of marble that took six guys to carry in here. And we're talking about cars and licenses anyway."

"You think this stuff *means* anything? This is my parents' stuff. When I leave here, it stays with them. I'm probably going to go into the Peace Corps or Teach for America or something and live in a ratty apartment and eat ramen noodles. I just happen to have this car right now that you could just happen to drive so I don't have to drive the whole time there and back. Whose stuff is whose doesn't matter."

"Jeez, Chels, can you just *drop* it? I don't want to, okay? 'Whose stuff is whose doesn't matter' is the kind of condescending bullshit only people who have money say, first off. And second off, not everyone wants to drive around in a BMW terrorizing old ladies, okay?" As soon as I say it, I regret it. I'm such an idiot. It comes out so much meaner than I intended it to sound.

"Okay, fine, M, fine. I just thought it would be fun sharing the driving. You don't have to be snippy."

"I'm sorry," I say.

"Forget it."

CHAPTER NINE

One of the many good things about Chelsea is that after the very few times we've had a fight, she is over it fast. Like it never happened. Plus, Chelsea is Excited with a capital E about this college visit. After school on the Thursday of the drive, Chelsea is like a kindergartener who has just gotten a bag full of candy. I feel like I'm about to take a whole lot of gross-tasting medicine. For three straight days.

"Okay, I've gotten an oil change, had the tires rebalanced, my phone's fully charged, I have my car charger, jeans, a skirt, makeup, road trip food. Have I forgotten anything?"

We've had this conversation eighteen times in the last week, and given the NASA-level charts and checklists she's compiled, I doubt it.

"Pepper spray?"

"M.T., you must be excited. Why are you being such a downer?"

Once we hit the road, though, it kind of is fun. Route 95 curves wide and unlovely in front of us as we head north, across the stop-and-crawl George Washington Bridge traffic and into New York State. The leaves are turning and the radio is playing good music. Chelsea is driving slow by the rules of the Chelsea-verse, keeping on the right side of the road and holding the wheel with both hands.

"Siobhan kicked out one of her roommates so we could bunk with her. Not sure about the other one. You and I can share the one bunk if we have to."

"Okay."

"And she says there's some kind of frat party we should go to."

Not excited about the frat party.

"And Siobhan is going to her Women in Antiquity class tomorrow if you want to go with her. She asked her professor and it's okay."

"We'll see."

"We'll see," Chelsea says mockingly, trying to get me to laugh. I know I am being un-fun, but I can't seem to get into it.

Chelsea waits until we're almost at the Connecticut border to ask, "So what's with the no college thing, M?"

Uh-oh.

"I don't know."

"You're going to Argentina and you don't want to tell me, right?"

"No! Wait, what?"

"I've been scared about that since you said you weren't going to college."

"Where did that come from?"

"Well, you always used to say that."

"I did not."

"Of course you did. At the end of every school year. Starting in kindergarten. Don't you remember? You would say good-bye because you were going to live in your . . . it was something about an oval house or something? Do they make houses oval over there?"

"God, Chels, no. My dad had this crazy idea about building us a round house. *La Casa Redonda*, he called it. And that was like a million years ago. When was the last time you heard me say that? I only said that because my dad would tell me to say good-bye to all my friends because we were moving away."

"I don't know, you looked pretty happy about it."

"I did not. I was a dumb kid anyway."

"What ever happened with that business your parents were building in Argentina?"

"I don't know."

"You always told me they were sending all their money over there and that's why you couldn't . . ." Suddenly she looks embarrassed. She just says, "Remember?"

"No." But that's a lie. I do remember.

When I was little, my father would come home and hand his tips over to my mother. Before they started cutting off the electricity. Before my father started staying away more and more hours. Before he started walking in through the door like his feet weighed a ton. Back then, my mother would take his tips and put them in a big old metal box that was drilled into the wall in a kitchen cabinet, because my mother said thieves never looked in the kitchen. The box was hidden behind bags of lentils and some cans.

One day, my mother and father took all the money out of the box and handed it over to their friend, whom I called Tio Roberto. He used to come over for dinner every Sunday and they would talk for hours about the business they would build back home. Tio Roberto was going to be their partner. The business would make us all rich and would help us move back to be with the family my parents always missed so much.

It must have been about a year after that when I walked into the kitchen to see my father holding his head in his hands, his elbows on the chipping table, my mother's arms around him. I must have been about nine, because I remember it was one of the first times I was allowed to walk home from school alone.

"What happened, Ma?"

"Nothing," said my father.

"We might as well tell her, Jorge." Turning to me, she said, "It's Tio Roberto and the business. Our business is gone."

"What do you mean gone?"

"Gone. Just . . . Tio Roberto stopped calling us and stopped answering when we called. And today we sent my sister's husband over to talk to him and the business was closed down. Just gone. Everything."

My father made a weird noise, his head still in her arms.

"But he has to give us our money back, right?"

"We can try, but I don't think so," said my mother. "I don't know what we can do from so far away if we can't even find him."

"Are we moving back to Argentina now? Maybe you can find him and make him give us back our money."

"We can't go back like this," said my father, muffled.

"Like what?" I said.

"We came here with nothing. We can't go back with nothing after all these years."

"Monserrat Thalia, don't worry about it. Go do your homework," said my mother.

And that was the last I ever heard about our business. But I don't want to tell Chelsea any of that.

She's still talking, keeping both hands on the wheel as a giant tractor-trailer passes by us. Chelsea says, "I can't tell you how many times I went home and cried to my mom about all the times you told me you were moving down there. And she always used to tell me that if you really moved, we'd visit you."

"I never knew that."

"Yeah, well, if that's what you wanted to do, I wanted to be happy for you."

"You're crazy. I'm not going anywhere." I wonder if I told her the truth now how she would react. I want to tell her. I start to figure out the sentence in my mind. But I can't get over the thought that she would pull back in disgust that she's been having a sneaky little illegal in her life all this time. That somehow I've infiltrated her pure, perfect, charmed life and made it dirty.

"Not even college, apparently."

"Ooooh, burn. Score one, Miss O'Hara. What's with all the parental college pushing?"

"It's just going to be so weird not being together next year. Don't you think?"

"Yeah. I think."

"Plus you're so smart. I just want you to . . . you know. Whatever. You force me to sound like a dweeb."

I poke her with my elbow affectionately. "To be honest, it doesn't take that much forcing." She laughs. "Come on," I say. "We need some sugar."

"Agreed," she says, as I reach into the backseat to the giant stash she brought and breathe a sigh of relief that she's letting us drop the school conversation.

IT'S ABOUT 6:00 P.M. WHEN WE FINALLY ROLL THROUGH THE huge stone gates. For a minute, it looks like we're really in a Disney princess movie or a medieval fairy tale. The buildings all look like perfect Gothic castles, tall spires reaching up past postcard orange and red trees. I love it so much I hate it.

The Red Bull I had on the way in the hopes of getting myself more "up" for this is making my heart pound. Siobhan is waiting for us in red Abercrombie sweatpants and a hoodie. She hops in the backseat.

"You made it," she says. "I'm so excited! We're going to have a great time!" I think I like her even less when she's happy. It's like watching a reptile dance.

Then she spots my Red Bull and points to it. "Do you love Red Bull? I love Red Bull. I don't think I'd be surviving college without it. You know?" Then she grabs my forearm and talks ten thousand words a minute like she's just had twelve Red Bulls.

At least someone will be jumpier than I am.

"So first, there's this a cappella thing that I said we'd go to. My boyfriend's in it; you can meet him. Then there's the party at Psi. But we can't stay out late because I've got class tomorrow morning. You coming . . . M.T.?"

Eeek. She's trying.

"Yeah, I guess."

"Awesome! You're going to love my professor. She's the coolest."

She shows us where to park and puts a visitor's pass on the dashboard, and we take the long walk to her dorm room. I've never seen a college campus before and it makes me ache more than ever to know I won't be able to go. The buildings are even prettier up close, with gargoyles and architectural details in stone, statues that look a gazillion years old. We walk up to a building with ivy growing up its walls—ivy, of course—and Siobhan leads us inside.

At least the inside looks like it's seen better days. It gives me a flash of wicked satisfaction. The overhead fluorescents are awful, and the paint looks as bad as any apartment I've ever lived in. The industrial-strength carpet is worn through in the middle of the path, mysterious black stains spotting it. Siobhan leads us through the maze, left, then right, no views of the outside world, until I have no idea which direction I'm walking. Then she stops at a door that looks like every other door, covered with a message board with things stuck and drawn on it. Siobhan's says: "Hi Cuz!!" and "Hello,

Siobhan's Cousin!" and "Study group changed to 11:00 tomorrow," and "Tracy let me borrow your charger. Come snatch it back. B." and "TB, your band blows." This last one Siobhan rubs off with her index finger.

"Home sweet home," she says, swinging her door open and letting us in first.

Inside, it's like you'd expect Siobhan to live if she got sent to white-collar prison for starving her slaves or something. She's got cinder-block walls, but she's made them fashionable somehow. There's a Monet and an inspirational quote. She's got very clean-looking white curtains. Her desk is immaculate, with color-coordinated accessories, like *Better College Dorms and Desktops* is on its way for a photo shoot. It's tight quarters, but everything is in matching Container Store so-chic plastic boxes of various sizes. You can see a mile away that she's gotten Top Bunk, because her beige comforter with tiny pink roses is neatly spread over it.

"Sorry about my roommate. She's such a slob," Siobhan says, kicking some shoes under the bottom bunk. The bottom bunk has a camouflage bedspread and a poster that says, "My karma ran over your dogma and your dogma had to be put to sleep."

I like the roommate already.

"Where's your other roommate, Siobhan?" asks Chelsea.

"The other one went home for the weekend," says Siobhan. Her ears flame red again in a flash and I remember the Spanish room-mate from the Bronx. Her bed is covered in a plain blue comforter that looks too short. A chunk of bare sheet shows at the bottom.

Siobhan and Chelsea are off and running talking about holi-days, dinners, family stuff. I take a minute to look around the room. I get a wild urge to put my nose up against her walls and take a long sniff, to inhale them, to suck this place in, to make it live in my lungs when I get found out for the imposter I am and get escorted off the premises, out of the state, and out of the country.

"So, do you, M.T.?" It's the first time I've heard Siobhan say my name not-reluctantly.

"Do I what?"

"Do you need to take a shower before we go out?"

"I . . . guess."

"I hope you brought flip-flops like I told you to. Those swim team girls are brutes with mushrooms growing between their toes."

I don't own any flip-flops. Maybe not so much with the shower, then.

"It's okay, M, you can borrow mine," says Chelsea.

We shower and change into jeans and T-shirts with hoodies. We're only a couple of hours north of the city, but it's way colder, and the damp spot in my hair by the nape of my neck gets icy cold on the walk from Siobhan's dorm, across the quad, down a path behind some buildings, around a bend, and into a building and a big, vaulted ceiling room. It looks like a church gone rogue, all the architecture but none of the statues designed to make you feel guilty. There is a fire burning in an enormous fireplace tall enough to walk into.

There is a little wooden stage and a bunch of uncomfortable-looking wooden chairs arranged facing it. A cluster of guys is standing between the stage and the chairs. Siobhan goes all "happy girlfriend" mode on us. "There's Josh," she whispers, like she's just told us the juiciest secret ever.

I can only describe Josh as a blond bear, with a big, almost squarish chest and beady blue eyes. It seems he is covered with blond fur. I've never seen a blond furry person. I associate furry with dark hair.

Blond Bear walks over and intertwines his fingers with Siobhan's effortlessly, almost like scratching his forearm. A couple of his friends follow him. They're all in white button-down shirts.

"Josh, this is my cousin Chelsea and her friend M.T."

"Chelsea." Josh nods in her direction. Then he looks at me. "Empty?"

The friends make that weird man-giggle that guys do. I know Josh is not being particularly nice, but I kind of like "Empty." I've never thought of that before, surprisingly. For all my stellar grades, I actually stink at word games and figuring out what initials stand for. I seriously think it's, like, the one "English-as-a-second-language" quirk I've got. I'm a little disappointed in Quinn "Is-her-name-Mousy-Rat" Ford and her crew for not coming up with this one.

Empty. It could mean a lot of things. Devoid. Unburdened. Without baggage.

"Yeah, it's a big, existential statement, my name," I say.

Chelsea says, "M. Period. T. Period."

"Oh, so you're, like, too T. S. Eliot to have a whole name?" says one of the friends.

"Maybe you just haven't scored high enough to hear it yet," I say, deadpan.

The friends laugh nervously, and one of them backhandedly smacks Josh in the chest and says, "Let's go, it's time to get started."

Siobhan grabs Chelsea and drags her to the front row. I follow reluctantly, only because I know I won't be able to find my way back to Siobhan's dorm on my own.

In a little bit, the white-shirted bunch gets up on the wooden stage. It's only about as tall as a milk crate. It creaks.

They begin. Some of them start saying, "A-wee-mah-weh, a-wee-mah-weh, a-wee-mah-weh, a-wee-mah-weh." Some other guy starts wailing, "Weee." All of a sudden, Josh belts out with something about a lion and a jungle.

I sideways glance at Siobhan. She's got a rock-star-is-in-the-house glow in her eyes.

There's an awkward retro weirdness to the whole thing. If I didn't want to leave so much, maybe I'd think it kind of sounds cool. It's amazing how they all sing different parts but sound like one whole song, almost like an orchestra of voices. But what kind of guy wants to sit around with a bunch of other guys and sing without instruments? If you can sing, shouldn't you do some kind of chick-magnet rock-band thing? Instead of this barbershop quartet, super-unhip gig? I glance around as much as I can without moving my neck to see if anyone is laughing at them, but everyone seems to be into it.

Strange land, this college.

I will always be a stranger everywhere. With my parents, I am too American. With Americans, I am a spectator with my nose pressed against their windowpanes, watching their weird rituals and rites of passage, never quite understanding them completely. A little chunk of me will always be a stranger everywhere, different chunks of stranger in different situations.

They do a pretty cool "Bohemian Rhapsody" and a downright sweet "California Dreamin'." Nothing from this century. Finally they step off the stage and there is some polite clapping. I am surprised at the little flame of "Come back" that jumps up in my heart before I remind myself how stupid the whole thing is.

CHAPTER TEN

Josh and a couple of his a cappella friends come back with us to Siobhan's dorm room to pass time before the frat party. It turns out it's some kind of academic frat Josh belongs to, so whatever visions of keggers Chelsea had are now being replaced by the reality of these somewhat geeky guys with the Blond Bear for a leader standing around looking awkward.

His friend, a mousy dude with a voice that cracks so much I'm sure he's putting it on, pulls a joint out of his pocket and lights it up. He takes a drag and passes it on. Siobhan holds it out to her right without taking any. Blond Bear takes a healthy dose. Chelsea has a little. She's not much of a smoker. I've seen it at parties and even had some once at Tyler's house (Tyler, female) after the class trip sophomore year. It did absolutely nothing to me, so I figure I can take a drag of this and it will have the same non-effect. So I do. It smells like fire pit.

I lose track of how many times it goes around, and then someone says it's time to go to the party. We leave single file, very quiet. I notice the spots on the carpet have some kind of meaning I didn't realize before. They point the way to something. They tell some story. I reach in my mind and can't seem to find it. Box. Violin. Eel. Beach ball? No, wait, Venus. Venus in the dark. It means something.

Chelsea looks at me, "M, you okay?"

"It's not cold like before."

"It's still pretty cold," she says.

"I mean, yes, it's cold," I try to explain. "But not the same kind like before, you know? Like, this cold kind of lifts your arm hairs out of their follicles and then gently puts them back. You know what I mean?"

She laughs. "I have no idea what you mean."

The Blond Bear walks over to me. "So you're kinda messed up, huh?"

"No. I mean, am I?"

"You don't smoke much?"

"No."

"What do you guys do for fun in New Jersey?"

"We hunt bear," I say. And laugh. Damn, I'm funny.

"Ha. I wouldn't have taken you for a redneck," he says. "Where in your toxic waste dumps do you find bear?"

"Where are you from, anyway?"

"Around here. Connecticut born and bred."

"Well, if you're into that kind of thing."

"I'm not, particularly, but I haven't figured out anything better. How about you? Have you always lived in New Jersey?"

"You're quite the census taker."

"Siobhan says you're Spanish."

"Does she."

"I'm a Spanish literature minor. Have you read *Bodas de Sangre*?"

I ignore this question. Instead I ask, "What's your major?"

"Classical Civilization and Latin American Studies."

"So . . . going for the practical stuff."

"My dad wants me to be a lawyer."

Maybe I *am* high, I start to think.

"So, you speak Spanish?" he asks me.

"No," I lie.

"Ah. Losing touch with your roots?"

"Yeah." *Trying to, anyway.* "You?"

"There's no escaping WASPiness."

"So what's with you and the Spanish literature anyway?"

"I spent a few summers building schools in Guatemala with my Unitarian church. Amazing. The Classical Studies thing . . . I just like old things."

Suddenly, Siobhan hops in between us. She freaks me out a little. I wonder if she sees me jump. She's still Red Bulled to the max.

"So, you guys are getting to know each other?" she says, hooking Josh's arm with her elbow.

"She doesn't speak Spanish," says Josh in an I-told-you-so kind of way. Sounding weirdly disappointed.

"I thought you did?" Siobhan cocks her head, reminding me of a cocker spaniel. A really red-nosed cocker spaniel.

"Nope," I say. And it's a good thing I don't have to explain the lie, because we're at the party.

It turns out beer goes pretty well with weed. I like that about it. I sit in an ancient wing chair, which might have once been nice, but now is covered in purple stains and a couple of spots where gum stuck and developed into a black blotch.

It seems that frat parties are events where three boys act really loud and stupid and everyone else sits around talking. I don't feel much like talking. There is a fascinating commentary going on in my head. It makes everything profound. Or hilarious. Or sometimes profoundly hilarious. Chelsea talks to Siobhan across the room, laughing, telling a story with her arms down by her sides but her shoulders moving. Siobhan hangs on Josh, who holds a red plastic cup and swigs from it. An emo chick makes out with a frat boy in the corner.

I hold my cup of beer and stare at it. A world of wonder, this cup of liquid.

I go outside to the balcony, drink my beer slowly, and relish being alone.

After ten minutes (or maybe two hours, I can't be sure), I hear the door to the balcony creaking. I look. Josh again.

"Hey," he says.

"Hey."

"What are you doing out here?"

"Staring off into space," I say.

"How's that going for you?"

"It's pretty awesome."

"You're funny when you're high."

"Okay."

"So why are you really out here?"

"Not a fan of the music in there."

"What's wrong with the music?"

"I've never heard of any of those songs."

"That's Hendrix playing right now."

"I don't even know who that is."

"Wow. There have been serious gaps in your education."

"No one I know has heard any of these songs. I guarantee you."

"So what?"

"I mean, this is not playing on the radio."

"Getting played on the radio makes songs better?"

I know there is an answer to that, but I can't seem to find it in my brain. It's like someone turned off some lights in there.

Josh is quiet, looks down the street. I wonder what his deal is. It would not endear me to Siobhan if her white-shirted, singing boyfriend were coming on to me. But he just seems to be talking.

"I think I need to mentor you musically."

"A bit soon," I say.

"And I think I'm going to call you Puffer Fish from now on."

"What?"

"Maybe Puff for short."

"What does that mean?"

"You puff up and get all spiky when someone gets too close."

"And you arrived at that diagnosis after three minutes of talking to me?"

"See what I mean, Puff?"

I want to laugh, but I'm certainly not going to give him the satisfaction. So I glare at him. But impaired as I am, I'm pretty sure I don't look too intimidating.

"Although, yes, I did turn into my mom just there," he says.

"How?"

"My mom is a shrink. You've probably actually seen her. She's the shrink on a bunch of those bad reality TV shows, addicted celebrities, that kind of thing."

"Your mom is Dr. Drew?"

He laughs. "Something like that."

"Well, I've got you beat. My mom is Oprah."

"The family resemblance is uncanny." He laughs, takes a swig of beer, opens the door, and motions inside with his head. I follow him in.

⤬

I WAKE UP TO SIOBHAN POKING ME.

"Are you coming to class with me?"

It's like she made some blood oath to Chelsea to take me with her and she's going to keep it, no matter what. I would absolve her of her duty, but my tongue is covered in cotton.

"Mmmm."

"Class is in five minutes."

I really dislike this girl, so I'm not sure why I want to do something just to please her, but I pry myself off her absent Spanish roommate's bed and hope I haven't drooled on it. For a moment it flashes in my mind that there is a Latino quota in this room, and with her roommate gone, I have filled it.

I laugh to myself a little. Siobhan looks at me strangely but doesn't say anything.

I slip on yesterday's outfit and pull my hair up in a ponytail. Siobhan is completely dressed and carrying a messenger bag. For a split second I feel like I've forgotten my stuff, but then I realize I'm just an observer. Someone who can look but can't touch. I don't need to take notes.

We walk in silence to class. I am grateful for two things: one, Siobhan has the sense to not try and talk to me. Two, the building that the class is in is close.

We walk into the room. All but one of the students are female, and the one guy looks like the class didn't turn out to be what he thought it would be about. I follow Siobhan to the back of the class—funny, she doesn't strike me as a back-of-the-room kind of student—and she finds two seats together for us.

I figure I should say something. "Why didn't Chelsea come?"

"My friend is taking her to soccer practice."

That shuts me up. I guess I've always known that Chelsea would go to college even though I can't, but seeing this place, so far away from Willow Falls, makes me get it in a whole new way. I'm almost mad at her, a little. Like she's betraying me, leaving when I can't. Next year, Chelsea will be starting the new part of her life. So will everyone I know. Only I will stay frozen.

I run the checklist of possibilities. Go to a lawyer. No, I know that's pointless. Go back to Argentina. That feels like being buried alive, somehow, going to a country where I've never lived and in which, by my parents' descriptions, I don't particularly want to live. Tutoring business? That's not quite right, but I can't remember why. My brain is still in stupid mode from yesterday. Note to self: no more weed.

As I contemplate this, one of the students gets up and starts talking.

"Okay, so, let's talk about the reading. The powerful role of women in ancient ritual. What did you think?"

Oh. That's the professor. She doesn't look very professorial, with a streak of blue dyed in her temple and baggy khakis.

People shuffle in their seats. No one seems to have an answer to her question. Heartwarming to know that people in college don't think much either.

Finally, one girl, a mousy one you wouldn't expect to speak, speaks.

"I mean, honestly, the first thing this does for me is makes me mad."

"Good. Why?" says Blue Hair.

"Because they never said anything about this in any history class I ever took."

"Well, remember earlier in the semester when we talked about peeling back the anthropocentric onion? Much of what passes for education on history is told through the prism of the male historians who could only see what they considered relevant."

"I don't get it," pipes up another girl.

"Tell me why," says Blue.

"Because it's like you're saying that there is no history. That there is no truth. Like, in this week's reading, it was all about how women participated politically through the designs they created on pottery in Africa. I mean, seriously? How can we even know that?"

"Anyone?" says Blue.

The first girl speaks again. "Because we've just been taught about what war happened when and who won and who lost. And that's not the sum of political and historical influence."

Wow, mousy girl. I glance at Siobhan's textbook, which she's quietly taken out of her messenger bag. I feel the wild urge to steal it. Instead, I memorize the title and the author. I bet I can get it on Amazon for a couple of bucks.

Another girl says, "But how do we know that this is any more valid than what we've already learned? That this isn't any more biased?"

"Of course it's biased. That's the point," says Blue. "Everyone has a right and an opportunity to explore things through their bias, to shake up and question what's accepted belief. We need to get out of our own Euro-American need to idealize the past and see men as competitive and competent and women as docile and domestic."

"I totally agree with that," says the lone dude in the class. "I really liked the part about the pot makers and how they shaped what people believed politically through the images they chose to represent."

Yep, that dude is definitely here to hook up.

"We have a student auditing class today," says Blue unexpectedly, jutting her chin out at me. Heads turn in my direction. "Tell me, guest, what do you think about the role of women in antiquity?"

I feel a tingle of electricity through me. "I'd like to learn how pots can be political."

"I'll see you in this room next year, then, I hope," she says. And winks.

I feel my eyes sting.

CHAPTER ELEVEN

get home to two things: Jose in red leather pants and my mother with a bruise on her cheek. On the good news front, the lights are back on.

I choose one battle to fight.

"What the heck is Jose wearing?"

"Aren't they nice? I got them from that lady who lives around the block from Chelsea, the one I made those black-and-white curtains for last month. Remember?"

Jose wiggles his butt from one side to the next. "I'm a rock star!"

"Ma, he can't go out in the street looking like that."

"Why not? What's the matter with them?"

"I'm a rock star!" screams Jose, louder.

"Yes, Joey, you're a rock star. Is *SpongeBob* on?"

"It's Ho-say!"

"Okay, how about that *SpongeBob*?"

"I don't know, let me go check."

Once he's out of the room, I turn to my mom. How she could be so dense is completely beyond me. I point to her cheek. "And what's that?"

"It's nothing."

"Sometimes I wonder why you don't kill him in his sleep."

"Monse! How dare you say that! He's your father."

"You could call the police, you know."

"You know what would happen if I called the police. They'd deport him. They might deport us all. I could never do that to Jose and you."

"Don't do us any favors. And they'd only deport him."

"Don't be so sure. Children need their father. And marriage is forever."

"There are places we could go. Shelters."

"And then what, Monse? Then what? They don't take people for longer than a few days. They don't take people without papers, either, I don't think."

"Then we could get an apartment. You could get a job."

"What job could I get? I don't speak English."

"There's help, government stuff. That lady on the first floor who always gives us her extra cheese."

"They don't give help to people like us. Without papers, you can't get government help. There's nothing. You're making a big deal out of nothing. It's not so bad."

She makes me so mad I want to shake her. How she refuses to

acknowledge how totally messed up our lives are. How she doesn't even see how things could be different.

She says, "Anyway, tell me about the college. What was that like?"

"It was stupid, Ma! It was boring! The people were all drunken idiots. What does it matter anyway? What the hell do you care how the college was? It's not like I can go."

"Maybe we can find the way," she says softly.

"Oh, because *you're* going to be a big help," I say, pointing at her eye. I know I'm being mean. And I want to be.

Two tears start down her cheeks, one out of each eye. It gives me a wicked satisfaction, like something I've said has mattered. I still want to shake her, but a little less.

She's quiet for a long time. Finally she says, "You still have that little cell phone?"

I didn't realize she even knew I'd bought one. Is she going to take it away or something?

"Yes."

"I have a calling card, but no phone to call on. It's my sister's birthday. I'd like to talk to her." *Quiero hablar con ella.* It's funny how things sound so much more personal in Spanish. I feel a little squirmy about her simple request of wanting to talk to her sister even after I've yelled at her. And I hate to think of her wanting anything. She never wants. It's like she's not allowed.

She asks me to dial it for her. As soon as I hear the funny long-distance ring, I hand the phone to her. I want to bolt, but she puts her hand on my forearm. Not holding me, just tractor-beaming me into position.

"Hello?" *Hola.* "What is my favorite sister doing on her birthday? Oh? An *asado*? Who is there?"

A barbecue. I have listened to hundreds of these calls, always just the one side of the conversation. But from the questions and the comments I know what the other side says. The people I've never met but am supposed to love. They are always having an *asado*. I swear they must barbecue for breakfast, lunch, and dinner. I see the emotions flit over my mother's face and try to study the paint that's chipping in the corner.

"No! You're kidding!" she's saying. "La Mariela went all the way from San Luis? When did she get there? Just to surprise you?" Apparently some rogue cousin visitor has shown up for my aunt's birthday. That's when my mother starts crying big-time.

"Oh, do you know how long it's been since I've seen her? Probably since that dance, you remember the one? I wore your green dress? And you were mad? Remember? She did my makeup and we tried not to let la Mami see because I wasn't supposed to wear makeup yet because I was too young?"

She is doing a great job at keeping the tear sound out of her voice. She has a lot of practice at that. Her hand is burning a hole in my forearm. I just want to get the hell out of here.

"Oh, *hermana*, I would give anything to be there. Anything. Who else is there?"

She's quiet for a long time, listening to the rundown of the *asado* guests. And then I can tell she gets The Question. The question they always ask. Every call.

"I don't know when I'll be over there, Mari Carmen. I don't know." Then she says the thing I've never heard her say before. "I don't think we're ever going back." And she's out of the closet with the crying thing, too, when she says that.

I feel a deep, drumming explosion in my chest, one where you know nothing will ever be the same. It's what I want, but it's not what they want. It is one of those wins that feels like a loss.

I don't know what her sister says, but it can't be good, because my mother cries harder.

I rip my arm out from under her touch. "Bring me my phone when you're done," I say on my way out of the room.

She calls after me, "But they'll want to say hello to you."

"Tell them I'm not here," I say. I am never going to talk to those people again. I bet they'll think it's all my fault that their beloved sister and daughter is never going home. That there will always be a hole in their family where my mother was supposed to be. It's one thing to know I am never going there. But it's another to know my mother thinks she's never going to get to go back to the family she misses so much.

A few minutes later, she walks into my room and gently puts my phone down on my bed. I snatch it up and head for the door. I can't stand to be inside anymore.

Jose bounces into our room again, doing the rock-star hip motion in his red leather pants. "*SpongeBob* in fifteen minutes!" he says.

"Not right now, little J man." I try not to slam the door as I go outside.

I ride around for hours. I don't even feel like calling Chelsea.

When I get back to the apartment hours later, everyone is sleeping. I stand in the door of my parents' room. I hear my father's soft snore. I look at him, my heart thumping.

I walk nearer to the bed. My father's jacket is draped over a chair. Millimeter by millimeter, I get closer. I slip my hand into his pocket. I root around for his money. I pull it out. If he wakes up now, I'm dead. Quickly, I count it: seventeen dollars. I grab five singles, put the rest back, and walk quietly to my room. Jose's sideways across his bed, feet dangling near the floor, mouth open, Sponge-Bob pillow in a death grip.

I put the five dollars in my vent. I lay down on my futon and stare into the dark. Only $170 to go until we're even.

I GET TO SCHOOL EARLY ON MONDAY SO I CAN GO TO THE computer lab and check Facebook.

There's an email from Nate. It says, "So, I was thinking maybe we could go to a movie on Friday. What do you think?"

Happy explosions in my ears.

In about four seconds flat I run down my outfit, makeup, and grooming decisions while I stare at the screen and reread his message eight times.

Then I notice a friend request from Josh, Siobhan's boyfriend. In the invite, he writes, "Puff, I can't let you be chronically unhip and parochial all your life. Accept my friend request and you'll know about songs they don't play on the radio." He also includes a link to a YouTube video by some band called The Smiths.

I click Accept. And make a mental note to check the word "parochial" on Dictionary.com because I'm pretty sure Josh just made fun of me for being Catholic.

Then I write Nate back. Yes, a movie.

There is a National Honor Society meeting before homeroom, and I close out the computer and run down to the lounge where we usually have the meetings. Everyone is there, sitting on the old, worn couches. Ms. North, who moderates the NHS, is standing up.

"M.T., I'm glad you're here. We've been waiting for you. There is some pretty exciting news," she says.

I find a spot to sit.

"So," she begins, "you know how the NHS plans a trip every year."

I have a feeling we have two different definitions of good news.

"I am particularly excited about this year's trip. We are going to . . ." She does her best game show cliffhanger moment. "England and Ireland!"

Delighted gasps all around as girls burst into little chirps of excitement.

"London, Stratford-upon-Avon—yes, people, we're going to sneak in some learning on this trip—and then three days in Dublin and a wonderful day in the Irish countryside."

I plaster on a fake smile, close my eyes, and pray for my invisibility ray to finally kick in.

"Dakota and M.T., as president and vice president, I'll need your help coordinating."

Awesome.

Ms. North aims her heat vision at me. "Is that okay, M.T.?"

"Of course." I smile. It is, in fact, the opposite of okay. No passport means no leaving the country. Well, I can leave, but then I won't be able to come back in. Wouldn't that make the NHS trip memorable.

She hands out brochures and answers questions. The sophomores chatter more loudly than everyone. It will be their first NHS trip. It would be my first too, if I could go. Luckily, it's not long until the first bell of the day rings. I get up to go to homeroom. Ms. North asks me to stay behind.

I know better than to pull the floor stare on her, so I look at her chin and try to make my look steel-reinforced.

"You don't seem thrilled, M.T."

"Yeah, I mean, England, kind of drippy, right? Not sure I want to go. I'll help organize, though. No biggie."

She fixes me with her I'm-not-fooled-by-you stare. "I know you have never gone on a National Honor Society trip, M. I don't presume to know why. But just say the word and I will make sure you have a ticket on this trip. We fund a scholarship and I—"

"I don't want to go," I interrupt her.

"Don't you lie to me."

I raise my eyes up to hers. "I can't go."

"I can speak to your parents."

"That wouldn't help. Even if they said yes, I still. Couldn't.

Go." I try to telegraph the truth to her so she'll understand I'm not being difficult.

She never takes her eyes off mine and I feel her running through the algorithm in her mind. I see a shadow of understanding in her eyes for such a split second that I wonder if she gets it.

"Okay, I understand. I'll make sure the teachers stop any efforts to persuade you."

"Thank you."

Her eyes play over my face. "I'll mark you present in homeroom. Go down to the locker room."

"Thank you," I say again. She knows what I need before I do. I sit in the locker room. I've missed other trips before so I don't know why this one feels like a bigger deal. I guess it's like the beginning of the end. Of how things will always be from now on.

I stay in the locker room during homeroom. I know I'm pushing it, but I stay through Ms. North's first period class, then Physics, too. I close my eyes and try to imagine Friday. And forget the trip.

Social Studies is my next class, taught by Ms. Cronell. Witchy old Ms. Cronell's class is harder to cut, so when the bell rings I head upstairs. I am not in the mood for her.

"Hello, children," she says. Her short, gray, filing-cabinet–colored hair goes in a weird, giant wave that's about to eat her head.

Children. Ugh. Just because she remembers the American Revolution firsthand.

"Now that we've had our last test on Reconstruction, I want to start talking about some of the forces at play in the early twentieth century. Let's start with immigration."

My left eyelid does a little twitch. *Let's please not start with immigration.* Not today.

"Can anyone name any famous descendants of immigrants?"

Is she kidding?

A hand goes up. "John F. Kennedy?"

"Yes, very good. The Kennedy family emigrated to the U.S. in the nineteenth century. Anyone else?"

"Rudy Giuliani?"

"That's right, Mr. Giuliani is second-generation American. Anyone else?"

I try to control myself, but I can't. I blurt out without raising my hand, "Ummm . . . everyone?"

"What's that, dear? Speak up."

"Everyone? Everyone is an immigrant."

"Yes, dear, but that's not what I mean. What I mean is who is a descendant of immigrants who came over in the big immigration boom of the late nineteenth and early twentieth centuries." She starts looking around for another raised hand.

"Why?" I ask.

"Why what, dear?"

"Why do we only want to hear about them?"

"Because that's what we're studying right now."

"What about immigration today?"

"Oh, it's dire straits that we're in today, I can tell you that."

Now I want to pick a fight. "Why?"

"Immigrants today are just not like what they used to be in our grandparents' time."

"How's that?" Heads start to turn in my direction. It is extremely not like me to get up in a teacher's face, little NHS, straight-A me.

"Well, they don't want to learn the language, for one," she says. "And they just don't have the work ethic. Just waiting for a handout. Take John F. Kennedy's grandfather, P. J. He left school at fourteen to go work on the docks to help support his sisters and mother, and died a rich man."

"And his son made his money in bootlegging and slept with movie stars although he was married, right?"

"Young lady, that's hardly relevant. What we're talking about is that our system today is overloaded and we can't keep taking all these people who are sneaking across the border like thieves in the night. If they could just do it like our grandparents did—"

"I'm not feeling well, Ms. Cronell, I'd like to go to the bathroom." It is a statement, not a request, and as I grab my bookbag, I nearly tip my desk over. I right it as I walk out of the room, fifteen pairs of eyes following me.

I go sit in the library and pretend I'm doing work. No one questions me. I don't know what else to do, so I fire up the dictionary.

Parochial—[puh-**roh**-kee-uhl]

1. Of or pertaining to a parish or parishes.

2. Of or pertaining to parochial schools or the education they provide.

3. Very limited or narrow in scope or outlook; provincial.

CHAPTER TWELVE

"So, Friday . . ." I say to Chelsea.

"Yes. We should just be at the mall and then you go meet him for the movie."

"But not with you? That feels weird."

"Yeah, we'll shop, then I'll leave and you meet him. But I'll wait in the parking lot for a little in case he turns out to be . . . I don't know. Whatever. In case you need a ride home."

"He won't turn out to be whatever."

"I know," she says, and squeezes my hand.

I write Nate on Facebook from Chelsea's computer. "How about the theater at the mall? More options."

The reply comes right back. "Sure. What do u want to see?"

"I don't know. The sappiest chick flick they have."

"Ummm . . . :-("

"Kidding."

"How about the alien movie?" he writes.

"With that guy who was dating the chick with the tattoo on her face?" I ask.

"I'm not familiar with his love life. ;-)" He uses a lot of emoti-
cons for a guy.

"Anyway, yes, I'll watch the alien movie."

"Okay, cool. Want me to pick you up?"

"No, I'll already be at the mall."

"K, see u there."

On Friday, I wear jeans and new shoes I bought on the strip
with my tutoring money. Chelsea drags me to the Macy's beauty
counter and chats up the makeup lady so that she'll do my eyes. To
keep her motivated, Chelsea buys three lipsticks and a stick of glow
lotion that costs enough to keep my family in lentils for a year. She
hands the credit card over to the woman behind the counter and
turns to study my eyes.

"They're perfect. Catches all the green on the edges, makes
them all sparkly," says Chelsea.

The makeup counter woman puffs up and smiles. It surprises
me. She's looked like kind of a hard-ass until now with her frown
and her harsh-sounding Eastern European accent. She says, "Perhaps some of the gloss? We have this wonderful new one that
makes you look like you've had lip injections."

My lips are inadequate. Of course.

Chelsea squints at it. "No, not the lip-puffers, M. They burn
like you just spread hot sauce on your lips. Which normally I would

allow as an acceptable price for cute lips, but not when there might be kissing in near future."

"You think there might be kissing?"

"Kissing is definitely an option," she says. She grabs a different gloss and hands it to the woman, who dabs it on me. Chelsea buys that, too. She turns to the makeup counter woman and says, "She's going on a first date."

The makeup lady smiles again. "He is a lucky one," she says.

I look at myself in the lit-up round mirror. I hope so.

We walk halfway to the theater and Chelsea stands in front of me. "My work here is done," she says. "You look awesome."

"You think so?"

"Yeah."

"So you'll have him drop you off at my house, right?"

"Yeah."

"Then you can tell me every little thing. I would hug you, but I don't want to mess up any of this perfection you've got going on." She waves her hand in a big circle in front of my face, then hands me one of the bags from the makeup counter.

"What's this?" I ask.

"The lip gloss. Some eyeliner, I don't know, a couple of things. In case you need to refresh."

"You don't have to do that."

"You can't show up there empty-handed. You have to look like you were having a busy day and then just happened to pop over to watch a movie."

"You're funny."

"Go!" she says, turning me around and giving me a little shove.

"See you later," I call over my shoulder.

I see Nate before he sees me. God, he's cute. He's wearing a button-down shirt, which I didn't expect, and a leather jacket and jeans.

"Hey, Facebook friend! It's nice to finally see you in person again," he says.

"Yeah, it's cool."

"You ready for some exploding aliens?"

"You know it."

He buys our tickets and waves away my money when I try to offer it. I watch him and hope he doesn't pick up on me staring at him. If he was staring at me that way, I think I'd feel it with my peripheral vision. But he seems intent on being nice to the ticket lady. Inside, he buys me popcorn and a soda, plus Twizzlers to share.

He hands me the tickets and picks up all our stuff.

"You want me to get some of that popcorn?" I ask.

"Nope, just lead the way."

"Okay," I say. No one has ever carried my popcorn for me. I'm in a little bit of a fog until I'm standing by the front row of the movie theater.

He wrinkles up his nose a little. "Do you really want to sit this close?"

I look around, finally noticing where I am. "No, not really. Just wanted to see . . ." I don't even want to explain that I was too busy thinking about how he was carrying my popcorn and being so nice to me and totally forgot to look for seats.

I walk back about ten rows. "How about here?"

"Perfect. You like it in the middle?"

"Yeah."

"Cool. You sit down and I'll hand you your stuff."

There is a little part of me that is expecting a camera crew to jump out and everyone to start laughing because I am the unwitting victim in a show called, "Did You Really Think He Was Being This Nice to You for Real?" But he waits while I take off my jacket and sit down before gently handing me my popcorn and drink and letting me hold the Twizzlers.

The trailers start and I have no idea what any of them are saying. I am throbbing with the proximity of this very sweet, very polite boy. I can smell the laundry detergent on his clothes and something else . . . what is that? Is that cologne? Or maybe just his deodorant. I do a slight swoon at the idea of him getting all nice-smelling for me.

This is a date, right? It's officially a date. It's only the two of us here. I shovel popcorn in my mouth. God, he must think I'm a pig. I wonder what I smell like. I hope I don't smell sweaty and disgusting. I hope I'm not breathing funny from my heart pounding this way. I hope I . . .

I finish the popcorn by the first explosion, right before the opening credits. I put my hand on the armrest. I feel electricity shooting from my hand to him, like those glass balls you put your hands on and the plasma makes shooting purple streaks to your hands. I can feel him, the cells of him. Can he feel me? He seems very cool and collected.

He moves his hand and intertwines his fingers with mine.

"Is that okay?" he asks.

Oh.

My.

God.

I briefly consider whether my heart will stop from all this galloping.

"Yes." I smile.

We hold hands for the whole movie. I have no idea what the movie is about. But that hardly matters. He picks up every bit of trash and walks it over to the garbage can when the movie is over.

THE NEXT MORNING AFTER COMING HOME FROM CHELSEA'S, I am sitting at the kitchen table watching Jose stare at his dry toast when my father walks in and says to me, "So I guess you're not going to school anymore." Almost like he's happy about it.

"What?" I say. It makes me so mad and scared I forget that my usual way of dealing with him is to ignore him all together.

"Jorge, let's not start with this again," says my mother, not looking up from the stove that she's scrubbing to oblivion.

"What are you talking about?" I ask.

"Those nuns raised the tuition again."

"Yeah, so?" I say.

"So we haven't paid them since last April. So they're threatening to not let you take any more tests until we pay."

I feel the magma rising up my legs and my belly and to the spot where my ribs meet in the middle.

This is not a new phenomenon, my parents being behind on tuition. In fact, I can't remember a single year of Catholic school that I haven't been called down to the principal's office over the intercom and given a letter with red late stamps to give to my parents. But somehow, they've always figured it out.

This seems different.

"I don't understand. So what's going to happen?" I ask. My torso starts to shake.

"Jorge, not now," says my mother, with a bit of a growl I've never heard in her voice before.

He says, "Why not now? What's going to happen?" Then he turns his head to me. "You're going to stay home. That's what's going to happen."

"It's my senior year. I can't stay home."

"Or you can go to Argentina now."

"I'm not going to Argentina."

"Listen, you better not start smart-mouthing me."

"I'm not smart-mouthing you. I'm telling you I'm not dropping out of high school."

"High school? What good is it going to do you? What do you care if you stop going to school now or six months from now? School is over for you. You're done."

"Jorge, if you just picked up another shift—"

He raises the volume. "No, I don't need to pick up another shift. What shift? There are no more shifts."

"Another restaurant, then—"

"Listen, I don't need you nagging me. And you." He looks at me. I brace for the smack, but it doesn't come. "You little spoiled brat. Demanding things." He turns back to my mother. "It's this country, you know. This country makes kids snotty and disrespectful. In Argentina, if you acted like this you'd learn really quick who's the boss."

"I'm not demanding anything." Maybe if I stay calm. Maybe if I reason with him. "I'm just saying that I can't drop out of high school. I . . . what would I do?"

"Oh, please, you don't need the garbage those nuns are poisoning your mind with. You can learn on your own. Education is not about school, let me tell you that. You don't need a fancy degree to be somebody."

"It's not that, it's . . ." If he doesn't get it, I am out of words to explain it to him. I consider screaming, too, but this is beyond screaming.

I go stand by my mother, who is scrubbing the stove like she's about to peel off the paint and find a treasure map under it. "Are you just going to let him do this?" I ask.

"Don't worry about this, Monserrat Thalia, okay? Go to your room."

I don't trust that I will be able to control myself if I start yelling, so I listen to her and go to my room. I am too mad to kick things, or to move. I look at Jose's SpongeBob pillow, the one I bought him with my tutoring money. He's written his name on it in marker on one corner. It makes me want to cry.

I hear the front door slam. I sit on my futon on the floor. I like that I sleep on a futon on the floor. It makes me feel like I could fold it up and carry it away by its handle. Take it somewhere better.

I get a piece of paper and start writing a list.

Towels

Sheets

Hair dryer

What else will I need when I go? It occurs to me that I have no idea what kinds of things one needs to live alone. Or how one goes about living alone. But I know one thing, something I've known since I was about fourteen. My days in this place are numbered.

Suddenly I see my mom standing in the doorway. I fight the urge to throw something at her. She comes into the room.

"Monserrat Thalia, I want to tell you something."

I say nothing.

"Remember I told you I dropped out of high school when I was in my second year?"

I stare at a puff of dust on the ancient baseboard. The model airplane sways softly in her wake. She must have bumped it on the way in.

"My father was sick and he couldn't work." By "sick" I know she means alcoholic. "My mother sold vegetables door to door. But it wasn't enough. So I got a job in the city. It was a good job, in a shoe store. It paid well. I bought us our very first television with my money from that job." She smiles, looks out the window. I glimpse at her, but turn my eyes away whenever I think there's a chance she'll look in my direction. "Even before I met your father."

She stops for a minute. I can feel her looking at me, but I wish I never had to look at her again. "I know we don't have much here," she says. "And I don't know what will happen to us. But I'm going to tell you one thing. Monse, can you look at me, please?"

When I do, her face looks firm. "I didn't finish high school, even though I always promised my mother when she was alive that I would go back one day. I didn't keep that promise. But I promise you this, and this one I *will* keep: *you're* going to finish high school. And I have a feeling you're going to do much more than that, too. Can you please remember this? Even when things seem most hopeless, there is always a way out."

Her self-revelation feels embarrassing, like I just saw her naked or something. I want to say, "That's stupid and a sorry attempt at a pep talk."

Instead I say, "I hate when you call me Monse. I especially hate when you call me Monserrat Thalia. It's a really horrible name. My name is M.T. now. You should call me that."

"Okay," she says. "But you have a beautiful name. Your grandmothers were so proud when we named you after both of them."

"You'd figure you would have checked to see if the two names matched together before naming me that. Or if anyone at all could ever pronounce it in America."

"It was a way to honor them. We named you for back home, not for here."

Ugh. She gets nothing. I just shake my head.

"I am going to fix this school thing, M.T.," she says. When she says it, it sounds like Emme-Tee. And then she leaves.

CHAPTER THIRTEEN

Sunday morning Nate calls.

"I wanted to tell you I had a really nice time."

"Me too."

"And so I know I'm supposed to do this whole masculine mystique thing and two girl days are supposed to be like fifteen boy minutes and I'm supposed to, like, not call you for a week to give you the opportunity to powwow with your girlfriends and ponder the inscrutable question of why guys are the way they are, but I thought instead I'd call you and ask you if you wanted to hang out today."

"Twice in one weekend? Beware the overeagerness."

"I'm eager, yeah. It remains to be seen if it's overly so or not."

"I'll have to check my calendar."

"Oh, good, follow the rules."

"Okay, I checked."

"And?"

"Meet you at Summer Park in half an hour?"

"Sounds good."

I run upstairs and take the world's fastest shower. I change into a V-neck Maleficent T-shirt, which I like because a) she's one of my favorite Disney characters, and b) it happens to show off just a smidge of cleavage effortlessly, like you aren't really meaning to show it, because, *you know*, you're wearing a *Disney* T-shirt. Record-time mascara and lip gloss, deodorant, shove the leftover gum from Friday in my pocket, deodorant again, and then off I go to the park.

Because he is on wheels, he makes it there before I do. It is an unseasonably warm day, and he's wearing cargo shorts that reveal some chicken leg action, plus a royal blue golf shirt that makes him look more adorable than ever, if that's possible.

"Hey," I say.

"Hey." He hugs me, and I feel the same sparks from the movies, but all over the front of my body. This guy is like electroshock therapy.

"Let's sit by the swings."

It's still early on a Sunday morning, and most people are either at brunch or at church or wherever it is that families go on Sunday morning. Plus, Summer Park is the less busy park in town, so if anyone is out with their kids, they are likely to be at the bigger and newer Coover Park with its giant fake-fossil climbing wall and enough swings to swing a small army. My plot is working perfectly so far.

I sit on the swing and he sits on the one next to me, which is a little lower than mine.

"You got the good one," he says.

"But my feet barely reach."

"I'll push you."

I haven't swung on a swing in, like, ten years, but the idea of him pushing me makes me tingly.

"Okay," I say.

He grabs the chains on the side of the swing, pulls me back, and lets me go. I swing forward, then swing back toward him. I feel his hands, strong, at the bottom of my back, close—oh so close—to my butt when he pushes me. I zip forward faster, higher, the wonderful millisecond of weightlessness and of knowing that I am about to start heading his way and he is going to touch my back. Then forward, higher. Then back toward him. It goes on like this, the dappled sunshine making me squint, the leaves brown on the ground, red and yellow and green and orange on the trees.

"Any minute now I'm going to buy you ice cream and take you home for your nap."

"You're silly."

"More swinging?"

I think he wants to stop pushing. "Nah, I'm good." I drag my feet to stop the swing. He sits back down next to me.

"So how are your classes so far?" he asks.

"Pretty good."

"Which one stinks the worst?"

"They're all an abomination," I joke. "I don't mind school, actually. Is that weird?"

He laughs. "A little, yeah. But it's kinda cool."

"How about you?"

"I do AP Math. Writing and stuff, not so much. I play tennis on my school's team. You like to play basketball?"

"What?"

"Basketball? I have a ball in the car."

"I . . . uh . . ."

"Weird, right? Weird thing to ask a girl on like a . . . whatever this is? I'm sorry. I'm not exactly smooth and . . . I don't know. Don't hang out with many girls. I mean, I know lots of girls, you know, but not, like, just at a park, just . . . I'm a little nervous and I thought maybe playing basketball . . ."

"I love basketball." It's not exactly true, but it's not exactly a lie. When I've played basketball in gym, I've liked it.

"Cool, I'll go get it," he says. I don't have a sports bra on, but I should be fine for a little bit of basketball.

We walk over to the court and start a game of one-on-one.

He dribbles to half-court. "What else do you like to do?"

"I don't know. I hang out with my friends. Read. Play soccer. Go to the movies. You?" He turns his back to me, and I press the front of my body into his back to try to snatch the ball. His arms are longer but his dribbling is kind of bad. I get it. Take it. Score.

I dribble it to half-court. I dribble right, then left—somehow I pull off a pretty good fake-out—then dribble to just under the basket and do an easy layup. He never touches me while defending. I catch the ball and throw it to him. He takes it to the half-court.

"Well, I . . . what I like to do is I . . ." He tries to turn and dribble, then turn, then the ball hits his sneaker and bounces away. "Damn, hold on." He gets it and tries again. I press against him to defend again.

"You are definitely fouling me," he says.

"Am I?"

"Ummm . . . yeah," he says.

"Take a free throw."

He stands at the free throw line. He makes like he's going to shoot. Every time he does, I jump up like I'm going to rebound.

"You are ignoring several key rules," he says.

He looks *so* nervous. He looks at my face and, for a split second, almost involuntarily, at my chest.

"Yeah?" I say. "Well, I think you're looking at my chest." And laugh. There goes my mouth, saying stuff before my brain can figure out if I should.

"I . . . uh . . . I . . . um, I'm sorry. I'm not like some perv or something."

"Well, that remains to be seen."

"It's just that . . . can I say this and then we will stop playing and never speak of it again?"

"Okay."

"It's just that they're really beautiful and I kind of can't believe and I . . . I guess I've never seen any bounce like that."

"Surely you've had gym class with girls before."

"And I have two sisters. But it's just that . . . I am really sounding like an idiot here, and you are clearly smart and fun to talk to and I don't think you're just an object or anything and I really want to get to know you, but . . . they are so beautiful."

"Just your standard issue thirty-two Bs."

"Fascinating and random bit of information. Fascidom? No, doesn't work as a word combo. Anyway, now that I know your bra size, I feel like our relationship has gone to a new level."

I laugh and reach my hand out to him and he puts the ball under his other arm. We walk to the bench under the willow, all the way at the end of the park where the lightning bugs light up the little stream when summer first starts.

We sit together, and he puts his arm behind me on the back of the bench. I snuggle into the nook that this makes.

"I'm afraid I am not making a very gentlemanly first impression."

"Technically this is like your fourth impression, so I think we can start relaxing around each other now. What do you think?"

"I think yes."

I look at him steadily, and he stops trying to pretend like he's fascinated by the grass and finally looks at me, too. His eyes are green and I am close enough to see flecks of gold and a little splotch of blue on the left side of his left one. And just on the bridge of his nose, imperceptible unless you're within kissing distance, a smattering of little freckles.

"You're . . . you . . . I think you're pretty cool," he says. Delaying, I think.

"I think you're pretty cool, too," I say.

Finally, he leans in. His bottom lip is bigger than his top, so it grazes me first. He just holds it there, but then slowly he begins to plant kisses on my lips, then, finally, a little more. And although the lightning bugs aren't there anymore and it's cheesy to think about fireworks, the air is so special and sparkly and everything stops and is so still that it feels like the air itself is exploding in little bursts of happiness.

For someone who says he hasn't been with too many girls, he is an amazing kisser. I don't have that much practice either, unless that whole sixth grade hand-kissing marathon with Chelsea in her princess bathroom counts. But then maybe there is no such thing as good kissers and bad kissers. Maybe there is only finding someone who kisses like you do, and kissing each other, only to then find it breathtakingly good.

ON MONDAY MORNING, MY MOTHER GOES TO SCHOOL WITH ME. She tells me to ask to speak to the principal. I translate her request to the school secretary. The one who usually hands me the tuition late notices.

The secretary goes through a narrow door and closes it. She comes back and says, "Sister Mary Augustus will see you now."

I'd sorta hoped that she'd be busy.

I haven't spent much time socializing with Sister Mary Augustus, and this is a good thing. She is a linebacker of a nun, scary and top-heavy, and prone to nosebleeds during assemblies. She focuses mainly on the troublemakers, the girls who sell pot in the locker rooms and walk out of dances with monster-sized hickeys.

My mother and I sit down on the low couch in Sister Mary Augustus's office. She is about three feet above us, Buddhist lama style. I wonder if we are supposed to crouch and never let our heads get higher than hers.

My mother begins. "I'm sorry to involve my daughter in this, but my English is not very good," she says in Spanish. She waits for me to translate.

I do it, reluctantly.

"That's fine. She's getting to be a young woman, and I think she can hear whatever we need to talk about."

"It's about her tuition," says my mom.

I fight the urge to run out the door screaming. Instead, I translate.

"Yes, I've been informed there's a past-due balance."

"We can't pay it," says my mother. "As you know, we're illegals and we can't get very good jobs."

I stare at my mother, jaw slack. "Ma, I can't say that," I say to her in Spanish.

She stiffens up her spine and says to me, "You tell her what I said." I haven't heard my mother be that directive since the time I used her best lipstick to draw in the hallway and she made me clean every last inch of it.

So I translate.

"Yes, I've imagined there are some challenges at home."

My mother continues, "My husband says we should pull her

out of school. She can't go to college anyway, so he figures there's not that big a difference whether she stops now or in six months. I disagree."

"Me too. I couldn't disagree more. She is one of our brightest students. It is unacceptable to not send her to school."

"I know," says my mother. "So what can we do about it?"

"I'm not sure. It's hardly fair that I let her attend for free when other families are also struggling in these economic times—"

"I could work for you," blurts out my mother. I can see by the look on her face that she's surprised that even came out of her mouth. Working outside the home is a big no-no for her. More accurately, her working outside the home is a big no-no as far as my father is concerned.

"Well, that's an interesting idea."

"I know how to sew. I'm very good at cleaning. I could do odd jobs around the convent. And the schools." The nuns run my high school and a small coed elementary school across the street.

"Yes, I think we could work something out. You can cover her tuition that way."

"And my son's, too," says my mother. "At the grammar school. He'll be kindergarten age in the fall. He could stay at the preschool while I work."

Who is this creature?

"Yes, I'll have to talk to the sisters, but I think we can make this work."

Sister Mary Augustus stands up, signaling the meeting is over. Standing up, off the toddler couch, we're all the same size.

"I am very glad you came in today," says Sister Mary Augustus.

My mother smiles. "Me too," she answers. In English. They shake hands.

"Young lady, get to class." Sister Mary fixes her glare on me and I want to get out of there as soon as possible.

I walk out single file behind my mom, through the narrow door, past the secretary, out the office door, and to the entrance. My mother gives me a kiss on the cheek. As she's doing that, and I'm wishing for a natural disaster to end it all, it gets just a smidge worse. Chelsea is walking into the lounge, and sees my mother. And my mother sees her.

"Chelsea!" says my mother.

Chelsea walks over and gives her a hug.

"*Que bonita*," says my mom, running her fingertips over Chelsea's bangs.

"It's good to see you," says Chelsea, and looks like she actually means it.

"You come to visit me." My mother picks now to learn how to string a noun and verb together in English.

"I will," says Chelsea, and hugs her again.

"Ma, I have to get to class," I say in Spanish, and start to walk away.

"Hold up." Chelsea catches up with me and waits until we're out of parental hearing. "What was that about?"

"You know. Parents. I don't know."

"You okay?"

"Just some volunteer thing. And my brother starting school next year. I don't know." I can really be a terrible liar under pressure.

This satisfies her. Thank goodness. "So tell me the latest in Adventures with Nate." I breathe a sigh of relief and tell her Nate stories on our way up to class.

CHAPTER FOURTEEN

My phone rings. When my father is home, I turn it off and keep it in the heating vent. But this afternoon he's working, so I have it on.

"Hello?"

"Hello." *Oh, that voice.*

"Hi, Nate."

"How are you?"

"Good. You?"

"Have to write a paper about some stupid play I haven't read, but otherwise good." He laughs. I love his laugh. I'm pretty sure I love the grass that his pant cuffs touch. "So . . . I was thinking . . ."

"Yeah?"

"My sisters and I have some tickets to a Knicks game in the city. We have an extra one. Do you want to come? I mean, I figured since basketball is our sport and all."

"Yeah . . . sure, that sounds like fun. When?"

"Friday."

"Okay."

"Can we pick you up at your house?"

"I think I'll be at my friend Chelsea's after school. Pick me up there." It's not that I'm going to keep him from seeing where I live forever. Just for now.

"M, I wanted to tell you something," he says.

"What?"

"I had a great time at the movies. And at basketball."

"Me too."

"I'm really looking forward to Friday."

"Me too."

We hang up and I lay down on my futon, stare at the ceiling, and bliss out on replaying that conversation for hours.

THE FIRST TIME I SEE MY MOTHER DURING A SCHOOL DAY IN HER new capacity as cleaning woman, I am on my way to lunch. I know she's working for the nuns, but I haven't had to see her for her first few days here. They've kept her in the dim recesses of the convent, where none of us are allowed to go. My friends and I have to pass the convent as we leave our school building to cross the street to the cafeteria, which is in the grammar school.

I am walking in a group of NHS acquaintances. I spot my mother as soon as we walk out the glass doors. She is in old clothes, baggy sweatpants, and a plaid shirt. I glance at the girls I'm walking with, to see if any of them recognize my mom. They don't. No one knows her.

She's carrying a big bucket in her left hand, the kind that started its life as a five-gallon paint container. Now it holds a squeegee and what looks like a lot of heavy water, from the way my mother is leaning left while carrying it. She is taking little steps so as not to spill it.

She puts the bucket down and wipes her forehead with the back of her hand. She leaves a streak of dirt on it. Her eyes are closed for a second, and I have a wild idea that if I just speed up, I will be behind her before she sees me. But no such luck.

She opens her eyes and spots me. She smiles in recognition, like she's about to say hello.

I avert my eyes, pretend to listen to something Quinn Ford is saying. I pretend it is the most riveting thing I've ever heard. I stare at Quinn's flaming red hair and little pixie face. Her mouth looks as old as it did in kindergarten. I wonder if they're going to see a family resemblance between my mother and me, and ask me how I'm related to this cleaning woman. I wonder if I can shield them from seeing her by making myself taller, wider. Or by creating a diversion.

But I don't have to bother. She's invisible to them, like a lamp-post or the nun mobile parked in the driveway.

From the corner of my eye, I can see that my mother realizes I'm not going to speak to her, and she busies herself with her squeegee. I walk by close enough to smell her familiar scent. I can't tell if I loathe myself or her more. She is doing this gross work for me and I hate her for it.

Later that day at home, after school, she says, "I saw you at school today."

"Oh, really? I didn't notice you."

"No, I know. But if you do, you know . . . I just want you to know . . . If you do, you don't have to say hello."

There's nothing I know to say in response to that.

⬥

NATE SHOWS UP TO PICK ME UP FOR THE KNICKS GAME IN A BMW. Doesn't anyone get any other brand of car around here? Chelsea has put me through hair and makeup boot camp and I'm wearing a pair of her Prada boots. I run out of the house and to his car. He walks around and opens my door. He kisses my cheek when he gets in the car. I move my hand up near my face for a second, like I want to protect the kiss on there. His eyes look greener by the light of his sunroof. I resist the urge to stroke his nose freckles.

"So hopefully I'll look cooler watching basketball with you than having you whip my ass playing it."

"Possibly."

"It's fun. Have you been?"

"No."

"Oh, you'll really like it then. My dad's company has a box, so it's a cool place to hang out even if you don't watch the game much."

"So where are your sisters?"

"We'll meet them in the city. Emily's coming from Columbia, where she goes to school. Becky's driving in with her boyfriend. Plus I just wanted us to just hang out for a little while. How about we go to Meatpacking to get something to eat first?"

"Yeah, that sounds cool."

He makes two turns and we're on the highway to New York. I spy the familiar skyline in the distance. It has an air of freedom.

The first time I lied to my parents, I was fourteen. I told them Chelsea and I were going to study at some friend's house, but instead we took the bus into Manhattan. We walked around, ate Ray's Pizza, and bought Marilyn Monroe postcards near Times Square. I was hooked.

Now my parents don't exactly know I'm heading in either. But without a phone in the apartment, it works out. Chelsea is my cover.

Nate says, "So you're a senior at Goretti, right?"

"Yes."

"What's that like, only girls?"

"Hormonal." I smile.

"Ha. I grew up with sisters. I know."

"What's it like to go to a school the size of three malls put together?"

"It's not that big once you get used to it. You carve out your group."

"Yeah? And what's your group?"

"Geeky sports, I guess. Not football players, but, like, tennis. We golf, too."

"You golf? I didn't realize anyone under forty was allowed to do that."

"I golf with my dad. It's fun, actually. I'll take you one day."

I wonder how many interloper alarms would go off if illegal little me snuck into a country club.

"So are you looking to stay in a small school for college then?" says Nate.

I can't believe I'm having this conversation again.

"I'm thinking of taking some time off." I figure I might get this out of the way, and I'm practicing my new version of this story.

"Yeah, that sounds cool. I thought about doing that. Emily keeps talking about how great Columbia is. I'm applying there. So if I get in I'll still be around." He glances over at me. Is that him looking for my reaction?

I am filled with a burning to tell him the truth about me. I can't, of course. But I want to like I've never wanted to before. I want to be seen. For real. For the truth of me.

"What will you do on your year off?" he asks.

"I was thinking of being a dockworker."

He laughs. "Smart-ass." He puts his hand on mine. "I have no idea what I want to be when I grow up either."

His laugh makes me laugh. "Maybe a diamond miner."

He seems to like the game. "Ice road trucker?"

"Shrimp boat captain."

By the time we get to Manhattan we've talked about his sisters, his parents, my brother, Shakespeare, the Dutch settlement of Manhattan, and who makes the best James Bond. I am beginning to get why boys are so much better in practice than in theory. How is it that I didn't get myself one of these sooner?

We walk around the narrow New York streets holding hands. He doesn't seem to be in a hurry to find a restaurant, and neither am I. I wish we could just stay here like this, walking, never doing anything more, never going home again. We make a turn. The streetlights have come on and the sky is getting dark, the wind kicking up.

He stops to face me. He pulls up the collar of my coat and asks, "Are you getting cold?"

"A little." He puts his arms around me. My heart starts thumping. He pulls back a little and looks into my eyes. The green in his eyes is shadowed now, almost forest green.

"You're so pretty," he says. And slowly leans in and kisses me. I think I may just burst into flames right here on this little street. The kissing doesn't lose any of its goodness with repetition. A homeless guy shuffles by us and chuckles softly.

"Let's find someplace to eat," says Nate.

After dinner, we leave the car in the garage and take a cab up to Madison Square Garden. I've never been here before. I've seen it on TV, but you can't get a sense of how huge the crowd is. We hold hands to get through it. I like that Nate seems to know the way by heart. We step into a small room with big leather chairs. I never even knew there were private rooms in stadiums. There is a spread of food—wings, dipping veggies, shrimp. It's more food than is in my refrigerator right now.

A girl that looks just like Nate with longer, lighter hair walks up to us. It's kind of ridiculous how much she looks like Nate with a wig on. She is in jeans and leather boots and the most enormous scarf I've ever seen.

"Natey, you made it. And this is M.T.?" she says, smiling at me.

"M, this is my sister Emily."

"It's so nice to meet you. Sometimes people call *me* Em, too!" says Emily.

"That's cool," I say. "Nice to meet you, too." I am always looking for people's angles, but she just seems genuinely friendly. Which instantly makes me feel weird. Or, as Nate would say, awkweird.

"Emily, is Dad coming?"

"I'm not sure. Mom said he might try to, but it's crazy at the office. The Merger." She says it like it's a proper noun, and I wonder if someone is getting married at his office or something.

"Where's Becks? I didn't see her at home."

"She just texted me. They're parking." Emily turns to me, "You'll like Becky. Even though they're fraternal, it's like her and Nate are identical."

"I didn't know you were a twin," I say to Nate.

"I am the most interesting man in the world," he says, putting on the voice from the commercial. "How can you expect to know all there is to know?"

Emily laughs.

"Do you want something to drink?" asks Nate.

"Sure, a Sprite?"

"Okay. I'll be right back."

It's just Emily and me. I look out the big glass windows and see how the court looks somehow different than the few times I've seen it on TV.

"Nate is sweet," she says. I have never seen siblings around the same age be this nice to each other.

"He is," I say.

"He really likes you," she says. "He never brought that Naomi girl around."

I know I'm supposed to say something, but I have no idea what. I observe the speckles on the carpet.

I imagine for a moment that I could belong with this golf-playing, big-scarved bunch. It's so silly, of course. I put it out of my mind immediately.

CHAPTER FIFTEEN

stay out of the apartment as much as I can. Life goes better when I engage with the Parentals as little as possible. I like my other world, the world of Nate and his family and their beautiful house with the giant, empty wine jugs that are inexplicably filled with little decorative scrolls bound with leather string. And a TV whose sound fills an entire cavernous family room like you're in a movie theater. And how nice everyone can be to each other when they are happy where they are.

Just like that, Nate and I start meeting every afternoon. I'm not sure exactly how it happens. Suddenly he knows my tutoring schedule. Knows to pick me up at Cody's house on Tuesdays and Thursdays. At Luke's house on Wednesdays. Knows to swing by and get me on his way home from tennis practice on Saturdays. Chelsea complains a little that we don't hang out as much as we used to, but understands, too. She says Nate and I are "cocooning," something she read about in some magazine. We have found the little empty pockets of time in each other's schedule and flowed them into one so we can build an us.

I know I don't deserve him, but it is delicious to know he hasn't figured that out yet.

"Where to today, madame?" he asks as I get into his car.

"I was thinking a state dinner, perhaps."

"Or a skip across the pond, eh?" he says in a terrible English accent.

"Why do all your accents sound Indian?"

"Just lucky, I guess," he says. Puts the car in park. Leans over and gives me a kiss. A stop-the-world, nothing-else-matters-I'm-giving-my-girl-a-kiss kiss.

He gets out and puts my bike on the rack on the back of his car.

"You wanna come over my house for a little bit?" he asks.

"Yeah, sure."

"I want you to read my *Hamlet* paper, too. Would you?"

"Yeah." He's more of a math guy and I've started to enable him in his literature papers. Which I love doing.

I'm at the laptop, reading his C+-at-best *Hamlet* paper, when he puts a yellow Post-it note over it.

It says:

Hi. ☺

"Hi," I say absently, putting it off to the left side of the paper.

He puts another one on. *Hi*. Bigger smiley face.

"Do you want me to read this for you or don't you?"

It's just that you're so pretty, it's distracting.

I laugh. And put the third Post-it on top of the other two, starting a small pile.

How is the paper so far?

"Well, I think that we're going to need to come up with a better word than 'hootch' for Hamlet's mother."

I put that in for you.

"Very funny."

You are a 32B.

"Are we on that again?"

YOU ARE A 32B!

"Yes. You have a great future in Victoria's Secret."

Don't be ashamed to say you are a 32B.

"We are never going to get through this paper if you keep doing this." And I put the Post-it on top of the pile. I love the idea of having a collection of his handwriting. I wonder if I can take them with me or if he will think that's creepy. As it is, they feel like a stack of demented little love notes.

As if reading my mind, he writes:

Why are you putting them all in a neat little pile?

"What else should I do with them?"

Throw them away.

Hmmm, okay, love note collection fantasy over. I make a move to pick them up so I can throw them away. He slaps another Post-it on the paper. It says:

NO! Wate! Then he scratches that out and writes instead, *Wait! You can keep them.*

"You said to throw them out."

I didn't think you'd want them.

"I do. They're your handwriting. Your, may I mention, really terrible handwriting. And you've never written me a card, so this is kind of like that."

Only better. Interactive.

I laugh. "Yeah."

So maybe I could say on these what I would say in a card.

"Okay."

I half-expect to get another 32B comment, but he writes:

I love spending time with you.

"Me too."

I love you, I think.

"You think?"

I love you.

This I don't want to say out loud since he hasn't technically said it. I put the last note on the pile, take the pen and Post-its, and write back:

I love you too.

We are about to seal it with a kiss when his mom walks in.

Her hair is perfect. She looks like she is a straight-up Ralph Lauren ad.

"M, how nice to see you." She says this like she didn't just see me yesterday and every day for weeks.

"Hello, Mrs. R."

"I've told you Maggie how many times now?"

"Maggie."

"Would you like some cookies?"

"Mom, seriously? We're not five," says Nate, a little annoyed.

"I know, I know. I'm headed out to the League," she says, like that's the right answer to Nate's comment. She picks up a humongous purse from the island without missing a stride. Nate obviously knows what that means, but I vaguely wonder if she's secretly in the Justice League. With her trainer-toned arms, I would not doubt it at all.

"Natey, sweetie, Carmen left some stew in the fridge. M, of course you're welcome to have dinner as well. And if you change your mind about the cookies, she made these amazing ones from scratch. If I don't watch out that woman will make me gain a hundred pounds." She pats her abs of steel.

"Oh, and Natey, the decorator may be sending someone over to do some measurements. Just let them in to do their thing."

"Okay, Mom."

She stops to give Nate a kiss on the top of his head, the first time this whirlwind of a woman seems perfectly still.

"What about Becky?" says Nate.

"She's having dinner at Jackson's. Carmen is in her room downstairs if you need her. Or you can text me."

As his mother heads for the front door, Nate flashes me a wicked-looking little I-think-we're-alone-now conspiracy look. He stands quietly, ear cocked like a bloodhound, waiting as the sound of his mother's Range Rover fades out of earshot.

Then he grabs me, throws me over his shoulder, and carries me over to the super-plush couch in his family room. He's kind of skinny, so I am amazed he's that strong. It's dark in the family room. There is only the light from one of the three massive Christmas trees that have magically gone up in his house in the week since Thanksgiving. Without sisters, maids, mother, mother's friends, neighbors, and decorators running around, we are alone. We have never had the house to ourselves this way before.

He puts on *It's a Wonderful Life.*

"This movie is, like, a hundred years old," I say.

"I know, it's awesome. It's my favorite."

"I didn't remember it was in color."

"No, it's just some colorized version."

But I see he just wanted the movie for background noise. As soon as the credits start, he's on me. He kisses me slowly at first, just lips on lips, so soft, then a little wet, then his breath getting quicker and his hands, stronger than I remember them, on my back. Just the small of my back. I arch my back to get him to go further, but he doesn't. Jimmy Stewart is on the screen talking to some whiny old guy.

I know I won't go further than this. But I want him to try so I can turn him down. So I can toy with the idea, feel the energy of its temptation coursing through me. So I can move his hand off. But he doesn't try anything. Just that kissing, that intoxicating kissing, my hands in his hair, the tips of his fingers tucked into the tops of my jeans, his lips on my neck.

He stops abruptly, seeming nervous. I look around, wondering if we're busted. He inhales in slowly, lets it out slowly. There is no sound but Jimmy Stewart making noise on some snowy bridge.

"M, I just wanted to . . . I wanted to say something."

"What?"

"I thought it was . . . well, I wanted to . . ." He stops. I guess he knows he's babbling.

"What?"

"Yes, I'm okay. I just . . . this is really nice," he says.

"And?"

"I love you."

"It's harder to say than to write, right?"

"I believe that the correct response is, 'I love you, too.'"

"I do. I do love you, too."

I have, in the weeks leading up to this moment, conducted extensive Google research on how to get boys to do what you want. How to get them to love you. I can't imagine that this beautiful, rich, sweet, good boy would love me, but I've prepared just in case. I have read up on who is supposed to say "I love you" first. Who is supposed to start The Talk. If you don't want to be the needy chick, I have learned, you're supposed to let guys take the lead in all that. Waiting has been excruciating.

So I have choked it back 1,001 times. I have doodled his name on my notebook. I have stared off into space replaying every word he's ever said to me for hours on end. I've tried to act cool when my heart was pounding out of my chest because he has forgotten to call to say good night. It's been two months. I have bitten my tongue, and I can tell right now that it's worked.

"It is nice," I say. Calm enough. Yes?

"I just want, I mean . . . I want it to be just you and me. I don't want to be with anyone else. I haven't been, since we met."

"Me neither," I say. "I mean, me too."

"I've always wanted a girlfriend. I'm not one of those guys. I . . ."

He stops and stares at the Christmas tree for a long time. I snuggle up in the crook of his arm where I fit so perfectly.

"My *parents* met in high school," he says.

I don't know what to say to that. I'm not sure how it's relevant. I wish we had left it at "I love you." "I love you" just deals with this moment and doesn't try to stretch it into the future. I have no future, so I don't want him making any comparisons to his parents in his head. I know we'll never be like his parents, that this whole "illegal" problem makes my future and his future very different. And that boys like him don't mingle their futures with futures like mine. But I don't have the heart to tell him.

He's sitting right next to me, but a part of me hurts like he's already gone.

I tell him it's time to drive me home. He does, smiling and chattering the whole time. Like he feels like we've crossed a bridge. I think we have too, but I suspect we've each crossed a different one. He's gotten himself a girlfriend. I've gotten myself a down payment on a heartbreak. I'm a little mad he really doesn't have a clue.

CHAPTER SIXTEEN

I go down to the strip, pumping my legs hard, feeling the cold air on my face. I look at the lit-up giant candy canes and wreaths hanging from the streetlights.

I'm making the loop to go back home when I see a man who looks like my father sitting in the coffee shop, reading a book. It can't be my father, because he's working. But the resemblance is so strong I go around the block to do another pass. As I ride by more slowly and closer, I make out my father's jacket hanging over the sidearm of the puffy chair. The ratty one I snatch singles out of.

My heart starts pounding. What is he doing? I park my bike out of his line of sight and watch him from an angle. I crouch that way for ten minutes, heart pounding, my breath condensing in the cold air.

Finally, I can't take it anymore. I march across the street and push the door to the coffee shop so hard that it slams against the wall.

My father looks up, shocked, and closes his book, *The Rise and Fall of the Third Reich*.

"What are you doing?" I ask.

"Reading," he says.

"I can see you're reading. I mean, why aren't you working?"

"I . . . I couldn't go."

"What does that mean, you couldn't go? Did you get fired or something?"

"No, I didn't get fired. I just couldn't make myself . . . I couldn't go."

"I don't understand what that means." I can't believe he's speaking so softly.

He glances sideways at the floor. "No, you wouldn't understand."

"How can you just not go to work?"

"I go. I just couldn't go today. I just wanted to . . ."

"You wanted to what?"

"I don't know how to explain it to you."

"Explain what? Explain that you're lazy? And selfish? Jose needs clothes besides those hideous hand-me-downs that people give us. I need money for school. We need food besides lentils."

"Your mother seems to be figuring all that out."

"Is that what this is? Because she's working? Or have you been doing this for a long time? Is this why we're always getting kicked out of our apartments?" I point to his book like it's dirty. I notice it's from the library. He probably couldn't afford to buy it if he wanted to.

Normally if I talked to him like this we'd be three smacks in by now. But I'm towering over him and he looks tired.

"Are you going to tell your mother?" he asks.

"Am I going to tell her what? That you're a coward? That you're sitting here in a coffee shop reading instead of hustling and building a future for us?"

"That's all done now. You've got to figure out your own future."

It knocks the wind out of me—not that I'm on my own, but that he knows it, too.

I fish around for the most hurtful thing I can think of. I don't come up with much. "I wish you'd had the imagination to at least be at a bar. But you're sitting here . . . what? *Reading?* That's your big try for freedom?" I turn to walk away and say over my shoulder. "You're pathetic." The barista stares at me. The cold air feels good when it hits me outside.

I pedal all the way home, as fast as I can.

I run up the stairs two at a time. I walk into the kitchen fast, out of breath.

"Monse!" says Jose at the top of his lungs and runs face-first into me.

"Hey, little man."

"Do you want something to eat?" says my mom.

"Ma, where's Dad?"

"Working," she says.

I want to shake her, but somehow I can't make myself even tell her.

"Monserrat, I wanted to ask you about something."

"What?" I say.

"How are things with that boy?" she says. *Boom.* That knocks some of the anger out of me.

"What boy?" I try to sound calm and curious, running down the inventory in my mind of how I might have been busted.

"The boy you're seeing," she says.

"I don't know what you—"

"Is he nice?"

I consider how much denial to get into. Sometimes that makes it worse. "How do you know?"

"I've seen you. After school. Once I rode by on the bus in front of the diner. And you're never home."

"He's just a friend."

"He's not just a friend."

I sit quietly for a while. "Yes, he's nice."

"Are you boyfriend and girlfriend?"

"It's different here than in Argentina."

"But are you?"

"I guess."

"I'm glad you have someone that makes you happy. You deserve that."

Her cloying at me makes me go want to scrub my skin.

"You know, getting married might be one way out of this for you," she says.

"What do you mean?" I say.

"Marrying an American."

"That's really disgusting. Getting married for the papers? Seriously, Ma?"

"I mean, only if you really loved him, not if you . . ."

But I don't hear the end of that sentence. I don't want to hear it. It ruins everything to even think of love as a something I'd use to get out of this mess.

"LADIES, I HAVE SOMETHING TO TELL YOU."

We all freeze. Please, not another eight-page paper. Ms. North's the kind of sadist who would give us one over the break, just because life is unfair like that and she wants us ready for it.

"I've accepted a position at another school. I won't be coming back after the break."

I start to vibrate like I've just been hit with the cartoon frying pan. I must have heard her wrong.

To my total horror, I start slobbering immediately. The more I try to stop, the harder the tears come.

Quinn Ford turns around and stares at me.

Ms. North keeps talking, but I have no idea what she's saying. I hear something about "successor is a great teacher," and college, and email addresses. I can't hear her. My sobs have gotten so loud more people turn around.

Already I've started to feel the utter pointlessness of continuing to try in school when there is no hope of any more school in my future. I finally understand the question: *when am I going to need this in real life?* Passing school is *not* real life when you are going to go on to a life where what you think and what you know don't matter. It might be for Mack and Chelsea and everyone else here, but not for me. What will all these books and theories and equations matter when I am scrubbing toilets or when I am deported to Argentina and learning a whole new way of doing things from scratch in a country I've never been?

My universe has only a few lights in it, and a big one just went out. I feel stupid for feeling this way about a teacher. I'd just stop seeing her at the end of the year anyway. But her leaving feels tragic in a way I can't even explain to myself.

I get up and run out of the class. Ms. North calls after me but I am in a full-on run. I keep going down the stairs, out the front door, and to my bike. It is the last half day before Christmas break, the day of our party, of our secret Santa. I've forgotten my gloves, and my hands freeze on the handlebars. But I just can't go back.

Maybe my father is right after all. Maybe I should just stop going to school now.

None of my friends are around and I can't think of anywhere to go. So I go home.

I sit in the kitchen. It's hot but not like the way it is in my room. I should be safe for hours. Around the holidays, my father's restaurant gets busier so he is rarely around. My mother, home early from her job and making some concoction on the stove, is luckily not in the mood to chat. I should have peace for a while.

Except . . . is that the front door? In the middle of the morning? It seriously can't be.

He comes into the kitchen. I prep for a fight. He is usually mean as hell around the holidays and it can't be good if he is home at this hour.

But he looks pale. And something else I can't quite identify. Scared maybe. He sits down at the table like he doesn't have any wind left. I see his left hand shaking.

"What is it, Jorge?" says my mom.

"Can you get me some water, please?"

Please?

"What is it?" she says, handing him a glass.

"They raided the restaurant."

"Raided?"

"We were cleaning up. Immigration came in the front and back. Sealed off all the exits."

"Oh my God, Jorge!"

My heart starts to pound. He sucks, but I know we can't get along without his measly tips. Did they just let him come home to get some clothes or something? Are they guarding the door? I listen. I think I hear someone outside. Maybe Immigration is raiding our apartment next. Or maybe he's led them here. Turning us all in for the free airplane ride to Argentina. *Maybe this is it.*

"They put us in the banquet room."

"How did you get out?"

"They interrogated us one by one. I had my fake papers, you know, that photocopy I have."

"Yes."

"Somehow that worked. I don't know. I think it was because my English is pretty good. I'm convincing. Plus it was crazy. Men with guns everywhere. The women crying. They gave me some notice to appear, but since the papers don't have my real name or address on them, I think we're okay."

"You're sure no one followed you?"

"No. I mean . . . I don't think they'd do that."

"How did you get out?"

"They just let me go. I don't know. But so many others . . ."

"Who?"

"Everyone. The whole kitchen. Paco, too."

"What!"

"Yes. I'm sorry."

"Poor Carolina." My mother's eyes water up with tears when she says her cousin's name, knowing that her husband is now gone, taken by the immigration people. I think of little linoleum-eating baby Julissa. Her father disappeared. Poof. Her mother making two hundred dollars a week cleaning houses. Julissa was born here, so she should be able to stay, to grow up in the country where she was born. The rules are that you belong where you're born. But it's not that simple.

"You're sure they took Paco? Maybe they let him go, too?"

"No, I saw him in a van. He's gone."

"What will Carolina do?"

"I don't know. You know having American kids doesn't save you from anything. I guess we'll help her however we can . . ." He puts his head in his hands, rubbing his face like he's trying to scrub something off. "We have to get the hell out of this country," he says after a long pause.

"Jorge, you'll find another job."

"That doesn't really solve anything, does it? Not *really*?"

My mother doesn't seem to have an answer to that.

CHAPTER SEVENTEEN

I stand outside while Nate makes the fifteen-minute drive to pick me up. I can't be in the apartment, and I don't want him to get any ideas about coming up. He belongs in one world, but this is another world. I know that the two could never be one.

The cold feels good somehow, making the skin on the front of my thighs numb. The pain makes me happy, like carrying something heavy makes people happy. Like you're standing up to the elements and winning. Although, of course, you're fooling yourself, because there is always something big enough to crush you, and a day cold enough to kill you.

All in all, I'm pretty relieved when he pulls up with his heated seats and pine-scented leather interior.

"Mademoiselle, your chariot awaits."

I think he's trying for French this time. "You still sound Indian," I say.

"That what I was going for." He winks.

He drives away, but not in the direction of his house. He takes a few turns and we're in the parking lot of Summer Park, where we played basketball what feels like years ago.

"What are we doing here?" I ask.

"I thought we'd have our own Christmas for a few minutes before we go to my house with everyone running around."

"Okay." I have his present in my backpack.

"I thought it might be nice to do it here since this is where we first kissed."

"Very romantic. But let's stay in the car, okay?"

He laughs. "Good idea."

He pulls out the most exquisitely wrapped small, slim present I've ever seen and hands it to me. I kind of don't expect it. I've never seen a present so beautiful, heavy with ribbon and a bling tag.

"It's so pretty! What is it?"

"It's normally customary to take off the paper to find that out."

"Wait, hold on. Let me get yours." I pull out the box. It's a personalized golf shirt, golf gloves, and a copy of *Hamlet*. The *Hamlet* is a gag. I've gone through and scribbled in the word "hootch" everywhere Hamlet's mother is mentioned.

"Go ahead, open it," he says.

"I almost don't want to mess up the paper."

"If only I would have known that I could have just gotten you a box."

I open it carefully, being sure not to rip anything, and lift the lid off the little box. It is a delicate gold chain.

"An ankle bracelet," he says. "Because you have such pretty feet. Or ankles. Or legs. Whatever. I just think this would look nice on you."

I run my finger on it. "Oh, and look . . ."

"M and N. You and me."

"It's perfect."

"But wait. You didn't notice the best part. Look at the inside of the top of the box."

I tilt it. It's covered in tiny Post-it notes that say *I love you*.

I start to cry. Because a day can have such different things in it, like Ms. North going away and Julissa losing her father and a boy sitting at his kitchen counter, writing tiny *I love yous* over and over again just to make you happy.

He puts his arm around me. "Hey, why are you crying? It's a good thing, right?"

"The best thing," I say.

WE GO TO NATE'S HOUSE. THE HOUSE IS STILL VICTORIAN CHRIST-mas perfect, but there is a vibe of activity, with Nate's mother and sisters and the maid Carmen running up and down stairs.

"Natey, sweetie, you're here."

I guess he knows that he's about to get marching orders, because he cuts in, "We're going to watch our 'Why can't I spend Christmas with you' movie together right now."

"M, honey, it's wonderful to see you. Happy early Christmas. Nate, sweetie, are you packed?"

"Ummm . . ."

"That's a no. Okay, we need to get that done."

"Seriously, Mom, it's going to take all of ten minutes."

"That's fine, you can do it after you take M.T. home, but then I need it done tonight. Not tomorrow when the car service is waiting outside. Tonight."

"Okay."

"And it looks like the presents I shipped ahead aren't there yet."

"Okay," he says, sounding like he's not sure why she's telling him.

"And the pet sitter is lined up, but I have an issue with the alarm."

"You're checklisting out loud again," he says.

"Yes, yes, you're right. I'm sorry. You go have fun," she says, turning around and walking away, clearly still checklisting in her head.

So we go to the family room. He picks up the remote and starts flipping through options. On Demand. Netflix. DVD carousel.

"Let's watch this," he says. *Sleeping Beauty.* I haven't seen this in like . . . I don't know. Ten years.

"It used to be my favorite Disney movie," I say.

"Oh, yeah, I remember the T-shirt. The basketball T-shirt. Is it weird and unmanly to admit that I loved it, too? I mean, until I found out that it was totally weird and unmanly when I was like four. Something about kicking ass in that thorn forest though . . . awesome."

"Okay, fine, let's watch it."

Somewhere around the "banquet in Princess Aurora's honor" scene, I say, "The good guys suck, right? I hate the good guys." I say this without thinking, kind of like you say, "Damn, it's colder than I thought."

As soon as I say it I realize it's *One of Those Things.* The things you think everyone thinks, or at least everyone under eighteen thinks. But instead it's like one of those observations you *think* everyone else shares, like, "Hey, isn't weird how everyone else's poop smells terrible but your own kind of smells good," except once you say it you realize you've gone out on a very long, very lonely limb. And they don't share it. Or else, they aren't willing to share it out loud. (True story, by the way. I once said that poop thing in third grade and it took until about the seventh grade for people to forget about it.)

So in response to my "good guys suck" One of Those Things, Nate just says, "What do you mean?" Blank face. Like . . . no shadow of agreement. Or even understanding.

"I mean, Maleficent is clearly the better character here."

"What?" He laughs. "She's horrible."

"She's misunderstood."

"She puts a *death curse* on a *baby*."

"I'll agree that her methods are sometimes questionable."

"Sometimes?"

"Look at how they treat her. They exclude her. They have this whole party and she's not invited."

"I'm pretty sure they have good reason for that."

"I'm just saying the villains are more interesting. You can tell that they've been through some stuff. They have things to say. They want things." I think that I could see baby Julissa growing up to rock a seriously Maleficent vibe. And who could blame her?

I go on, "Plus, don't you get the sense that the good guys are always bullshitting you? Like they're those kids at school that are absolute jerks but then act like angels when teachers are looking. These stupid sanctimonious fairies in *Sleeping Beauty* are just like those kids."

"You've given this a lot of thought."

"I'm just saying."

He reaches over to tickle me, "Were you, like, abused by fairies or something?"

It's in this moment that I get that he's one of the people who has no suspicion of the good guys and no twinge of recognition, no feeling of camaraderie with the villain. So I just let him tickle me and make me laugh. There's no cure for what he's got. I both envy him and pity him, with his impeccably dressed, checklisting mom and his boughs-of-holly-festooned life.

It's Christmas Eve, and my mother is in the kitchen making *picadillo* for the *empanadas*, as necessary to Christmas as a Christmas tree. Jose sits at the table, quietly having a fork run a bombing mission over some mashed potatoes. I sit and stare off into space. Nate hasn't called me all day, and hasn't responded to three texts. My father hasn't come out of his room.

I am in what one could consider a Bad Mood. It's made worse by the fact that my mother and Jose seem to be in such a Good Mood. Such a very, very Good Mood. Which baffles the hell out of me. It's like they can't see we're living in the real endtimes.

My mother actually hums. I despise her particularly today.

"Guess what the Nun said to me today," says my mother. "The Nun" means the principal, Sister Mary Augustus. It's like "The

President." You don't need to say which one. Although school was closed, my mother went in to work this morning.

"We're all going to hell? That's pretty much the only thing I've ever heard her say."

"Oh, Monse, why are you always so mad? She told me after we get back from the break, I can be an assistant in the *kindergarten* instead of just cleaning all the time."

"How will that go?"

"I'm going to help the teacher in the afternoons."

"Can you do that? I mean, can they do that?"

"Well, I think I've done a pretty good job with my own children."

"I don't mean that, I mean . . . you don't speak English."

"I speak a little. And it turns out that the kindergarten teacher speaks Spanish, too. And guess what." I am really not in the mood for guessing games. Luckily, she doesn't wait for me to guess.

"I'm going to take English class at the library."

"When did all this happen?"

"I just signed up last week."

I see.

"So I'll need you home on Tuesday nights." She's not asking, she's telling. I'm not sure I like this new and improved mother.

"Why?"

"You'll have to watch Jose while I'm in class."

I consider arguing, and root around my head for ammunition for about thirty seconds before giving up.

My father comes out of his room. He hasn't shaved. He looks like a wild animal, like one of the lions on *National Geographic* before they bring down a gazelle after a long, hard drought. All that fear in his eyes yesterday is gone and seems replaced by thirsty lion hatred.

"Hey, little snot, don't you say Merry Christmas to your father?" he asks. I say nothing. I believe the little snot is not going to say Merry Christmas to this guy. But I can tell that talking or not talking will all lead to the same thing.

"No? Am I too *pathetic* for that?" he says with a sneer. I can see that he will choose Christmas to avenge our little coffee shop run-in. Great. I knew about ten seconds after that happened that I would pay for it one day.

He stands over me. "I'm talking to you."

"I hear you," I say. Does that warrant a smack? I wait. Brace. Nope, not today. Not yet, anyway.

"Get your coat on; we're going to New York."

"Jorge, it's Christmas," says my mom.

"Yeah, so it's Christmas. So I want to talk to my family in Argentina. So New York is beautiful at Christmas. Can a man want to do something nice on Christmas with his family? Is that allowed? Get ready."

My mother quietly takes Jose by the hand and goes into our room.

I square off in front of him. "You see she's cooking, right?"

"She can cook when we get back."

"Why do we have to go to New York now?"

"Because I said we're going to New York. Who the hell do you think you are, questioning me?"

"It's Christmas. It's not just what you want. It's cold. How are we going to get to New York anyway?"

"I borrowed a car."

"You *borrowed* a car? You don't even have a driver's license. You want to be driving around at Christmas with a fake license?"

Smack. The skin tingles like a burn and my cheekbone aches. Even though I knew it was coming, it still makes me fist-clenching furious.

"You don't ask me questions. Now go get dressed before I drag you out by your hair."

I run down my usual options. Call the cops. No, get deported. Murder him in his sleep. Messy, very messy. Plus, get deported after thirty years in jail. Hit him back. Get my butt kicked, make the neighbors mad. Neighbors call cops. Get deported. I can't think of another solution besides sit here and take it.

I dig the nails from my left hand into the thumb of my right hand and concentrate on how that feels. I remember my list. Towels. Sheets. Hair dryer. *Add Band-Aids.*

"I don't want to go to New York," I say.

He gets up close to me. "Get. Dressed. Now."

My mother is back in the kitchen, a bird in a panic. "Monse, please just go get dressed. It will be nice to go into New York," she says. She's not convincing me. She doesn't look like she's particularly convinced herself either.

"I don't understand why he just starts making crazy demands and you just do what he says."

Smack. I dig my nails into my thighs, through my jeans. It steadies me, keeps me from doing what I want to do, which is hit back.

"Because I'm your father!" he screams. "Because what I say goes! Because you're a little snot who doesn't know anything. I have to work seven days a week, when I'm not too busy getting swallowed up in immigration raids by men with guns. And for what? So you can go to that fancy school and learn to think you're better than me."

"Actually, I think *she* works so I can do that." I know that's going to bring it, but I can't resist.

He hits me again and again, harder. My skin stings where he slaps it. I put my forearms in front of my face but that doesn't help much. I concentrate on not crying. *No crying.* It's one thing I can keep from him—my tears. One thing *I* control.

He hits harder, my ear, and it causes a weird tinny echo. Out from in between my lifted arms, I see Jose crying in the corner.

My mother raises her voice urgently, just under a scream. "Jorge, please! Jorge, it's Christmas. I know you're upset, but this isn't the answer! She's sorry!"

He pulls back, breathing hard. Hitting me must be hard work. "Somebody's got to teach her. Somehow she's got to learn respect. Kids in this country don't respect anyone. Look at how disrespectful they teach kids to be in this country."

"What are *you* teaching me? What! That you're stronger? You may be stronger now, but one day I'll be strong and you'll be weak. And you'll see what's going to happen to you then."

I think that will make him hit harder, but it doesn't. He deflates like at the coffee shop. I'm almost disappointed.

We go to New York. We come back. We have the *empanadas,* and, as always, we wait until midnight to open the presents. Jose is unreasonably happy. I guess ignorance is bliss.

Jose gets blocks and a SpongeBob filled with candy, plus some seriously ugly corduroy pants, but at least they have the tags still on them and they seem to be the right size. He sets off to build a pineapple house for SpongeBob.

My mother pushes two boxes toward me. "Open them," she says.

I do. One is a hideous orange messenger bag, the other a pair of jeans which I know I will never wear. But I know she's trying.

"Thank you," I say.

She opens the kindergarten craft book I bought her at the last minute and holds it to her chest like it's a couple of gold bars.

"It's so wonderful!" she says.

It is her only present.

CHAPTER EIGHTEEN

Christmas Day is its own usual blend of disappointment and jail. Nate is gone and for some reason he is not responding to texts. Chelsea is somewhere with family. Later in the week I'm sure I'll help her put away her whole new wardrobe and electronics and dancing bears and whatever other extravagant collection she's received for Christmas. And she'll give me the stuff displaced by the new stuff. We'll both try to pretend that she doesn't feel weird and I don't feel little and yet hungry and wanting at the same time.

Lucky for me, the Parentals ignore me. The thirsty lion parental now looks more like a whipped hyena, and is dressed and ready to go somewhere. My mother gets up to hug him. He kind of hugs back. I want to gag, but that would draw attention to me.

My dad actually puts a hand on my shoulder before walking out. It burns. It disgusts me when he touches me. I say nothing. I know this is his version of "Sorry."

"Good luck," my mom says. "I'm sure you'll get the job." I'm a little surprised that he's got a lead on a job so soon since the other times he's lost a job he's stayed in bed under the covers for weeks while the refrigerator got empty.

He just nods once and walks out the door.

After he leaves, my mother says to me, "I'm going to go see Carolina. Do you want to come?"

"No."

"Are you sure?"

"I'm not going."

So she goes out with Jose. I've got the place to myself. I call Nate, but it goes straight to voice mail.

I have this small, slow feeling of dread. I replay the whole night, the days leading up to him leaving. Did I say something wrong? The Maleficent thing, maybe it got him thinking.

I get an idea. I go downstairs to the Cheese Lady.

"Hi," I say when she opens the door, a kid wailing loud in the background. "Merry Christmas. I need to check a couple of things . . . reading list for school. I was wondering if maybe . . ."

"Sure, come in, come in."

The kid's wail gets louder.

"Pete, get up off that chair so that Monse here can look at the computer a minute." She says it "Munsey." Better than Mousy, but not by much.

"I want to play!"

"You're not playing, you're screaming! Now move before I . . ."

He gets up and runs away. The keyboard keys have black smudges and what looks like a dried booger on the *P*.

I don't want to stay long, but I feel an overwhelming need to go on Facebook to see Nate's profile. Cheese Lady hums softly in the kitchen, a toddler on her hip.

Nate's just posted a picture of himself with a whole other group of people I don't know. I look at the tags. Jennifer Whitman. Cousin. Daniel Whitman. Cousin. It bothers me to think there are all these people in his life that I know nothing about. It's already got thirteen Likes. I hover over to see who Liked it. A bunch of people from his school, a few names I recognize.

Then Naomi Ahearn.

Is that *the* Naomi?

I click on her profile. She has her security set way low, so although we're not friends, I can see everything, her posts, her pictures, her About. Under relationship status, it says, "It's complicated." What the hell does that mean?

I go into her pictures. Her making duck faces. Her with a bunch of her friends, a couple of whom I recognize from soccer or just around town. I look at her posts. Naomi is a fan of posting sayings like, "Rawr. That means I love you in dinosaur." I scroll past those.

It was Naomi's birthday three weeks ago. I skim over the HBs and there it is. One from Nate. "Happy Birthday, rock star!"

I feel sick to my stomach. Cheese Lady starts humming a different tune, something that sounds tropical and not at all Christmas-y.

I go back to her pictures, looking at them over time. Trying to go fast so that Cheese Lady won't catch me cruising Facebook when I'm supposed to be getting a school assignment.

And there it is, last summer. Naomi is in a bikini top and denim shorts, three cornrow braids on the left side of her hair, the rest of it wild and blond and beachy. She's standing in a giant hole in the sand. Standing next to her is Nate. His arm around her waist. Her arm around his shoulder. Her free hand doing the "rock and roll" sign. The caption reads, "Nate tried to dig to China for me, but only got this far."

I X out of Facebook in a rush and open my school's website so that if Cheese Lady looks, she can see I've been on it. I stare off for a second, sitting in Cheese Lady's messy living room on Christmas when everyone else has somewhere to be. And I am mad, or scared, or mad-scared at Nate, for not picking up the phone, for the whole aw-shucks, "I don't know much about girls" thing when he clearly knew plenty about Naomi, and for writing on her wall just three weeks ago. Maybe I'm an idiot. Clearly I'm an idiot. Clearly I made up that he felt a certain way, but here he is, writing to ex-girlfriends, not calling me. Of course what I thought we had can't last.

I get up and call out to Cheese Lady, "Thank you!"

"No problem, honey. You come back any time you need to." I run out the door.

I FINALLY GO TO CHELSEA'S. BUT SOMEHOW SHE'S ROPED US into going to Patricia's house to get ready for some party. Patricia's house is also Christmas Central, except her parents have done hers in an all white and silver. White tree. White lights. White ornaments. White pseudo-greenery going up the handrail of their curved staircase.

I am in jeans and a turtleneck. I'm a little less dressed up than Patricia and Dakota, who are both in skirts. Chelsea, luckily, is in jeans, too.

Upstairs in Patricia's suite—she's got a sitting area and her own bathroom—it's like the department store makeup area threw up all over everything. Beauty products are thrown around like confetti, on the bed, on the dresser, on the lighted vanity, and on several footstools. I see the bathroom out of the corner of my eye and it's similarly littered.

"Choose your weapon," says Patricia. "We've got blues and

greens over here. Browns over there. Blacks there. And all the hair products a Jersey girl could need."

"And the hot curlers and the flat iron are heating up," says Dakota, her toes in hot pink toe separators, as she takes a swig from a little silver flask. She points it at me. "Want?"

"Sure." I take a swig and almost cough up a lung. It's like kerosene.

"Patricia's dad has the most amazing fully stocked bar," she says.

"Awesome," I cough out, my voice kind of raspy.

"The plan is I have to look absolutely devastating," says Patricia. "Because Jason is home from college this weekend and he will be there." Jason and Patricia had a long and tragic high school love affair until he went away to college in North Carolina.

"So what's the status?" asks Dakota.

"I don't know. Off again, I guess," she says.

"Not if we have anything to do with it," says Kathy from history. She turns to me and asks, "So what's the deal with you and that guy from Willow?"

"Nate?" I ask.

"Well, are you going out with more than one guy from Willow?"

"No, I'm just surprised, because I didn't realize anyone knew."

"Ooooh, an undercover lover."

"No, not at all," I say.

"Your relationship status still says 'Single,'" says Patricia.

"Who knew you guys cared so much?" I say.

"Ha! Well, accuracy in relationship status is the new girl code, you know. It helps everyone know who is off-limits."

"I would like to think Nate is off-limits, yes."

"Why hasn't he updated *his* relationship status, then?" asks Dakota.

"I don't know. It's really not that important." But it hadn't even occurred to me until now. *Why hasn't he?*

I look over at Chelsea. She's flat-ironing. Not close enough to help.

"He's probably just still burned from what that girl Naomi did to him so he's taking it slow," Kathy says, then looks at me like she's reading my face to decide whether I know what she's talking about.

I don't.

"I guess," I say.

"I know, but to get caught with his teammate like that? That's just skanky if you ask me. Gross."

"I don't know her, but I heard from Laurie on soccer that Naomi is kind of known for general shadiness. Not easy, necessarily, but let's just say insensitive in her selections."

"Well, ladies, he's moved on, so we're all good," I say. I'm shaking a little inside, but I think I fooled them.

Nate didn't tell me that Naomi had broken his heart, and I wonder why.

I reach for Dakota's flask again and take a long, burning swig.

"TELL ME AGAIN WHY WE'RE DRIVING TO QUINN'S WHEN SHE lives five blocks away," I say.

"We're suburbanites. We don't walk," says Dakota, riding shotgun.

Kathy, the designated and totally sober driver says, "Plus these shoes kill for walking."

"But you look damn good," I say.

"Someone's happy," says Chelsea. She doesn't look overly thrilled.

We're at Quinn's in three minutes.

When we get there, I feel the low thud of music hitting the glass of the front windows and the double glass and iron doors. Some people are around the side of the sunshine yellow shingle house, although it is way too cold to be outside, and I hear a muffled crash somewhere inside.

"It's kind of trippy that cranky little Quinn lives in the hello-get-happy house, huh?" says Dakota.

"With her dozen smelly brothers too."

"There aren't a *dozen* of them," says Dakota.

"A shitload of them. More offspring than necessary for sure."

"That's a particularly insensitive thing to say. You know. After what happened."

We go inside and get hit by a wall of sound. Quinn's near the front door.

"Hey! Did you bring the booze? We are running low," she yells over the music.

"The parents were in full surveillance mode. I couldn't get any. I've got cash, though," says Patricia, stuffing a wad of bills into Quinn's hand.

"Okay, come in. Commence with the merriment," says Quinn.

Before I know what's happening, Dakota is off to find some guy she's interested in and Kathy is in the bathroom and Patricia is talking to Jason in the corner. Chelsea says, "I'm going to go say hello to Jonathan for a second. Wanna come?"

I know she doesn't want me to come. "No, I'm going to hang out here for a bit."

It's right at this moment that I remember I hate parties. And that none of these people are really my friends except Chelsea and she's just on a short loan. And that I probably could use more booze to get through this.

"So where's the bar?" I ask Quinn.

"You got cash?"

"What?"

"We're asking everyone to chip in ten dollars."

I am taken by the sudden urge to tell her, "You still owe me a silver crayon. With interest." But I don't. Instead I say, "Yeah, okay."

"So come on," she says.

I follow her out. She starts walking down the block.

"Where are you going?"

"There is a liquor store, like, four blocks away."

"We don't walk; we're suburbanites," I say, mirroring Dakota.

"Yeah, well, we don't drive drunk. Because we want to grow up to have pointless little lives like our parents someday. Walk faster. It's freaking freezing out here. Anyway, my brother has the car."

"Where are your parents?"

"Mom is with her boyfriend in Maui. Dad is with his boyfriend in the city."

"They're divorced?"

"No."

Oh.

"So what are you going to use for ID?"

"Shit, are you conducting an investigation?"

"I'm just making conversation."

"I have a bona fide New Jersey State driver's license." She pulls it out of her back pocket and hands it to me. It's a picture of her with the name "Grady Ford" on it. Twenty-two years old.

"How did you get your picture on someone else's license?" I ask. I'm a little in awe, actually.

"That's not me. That's my brother Grady. Can't you tell the difference?"

"No, well, yes, but I'm . . ."

"I don't look like a dude."

"I didn't say you did."

"You kinda just did, yeah."

"Okay, whatever. It's just cool that you have a license."

"Whatever."

We walk in silence for another block and get to a wider road, two lanes each way with double yellow lines in the middle. I wobble a little.

She stops at the corner and looks at me. I am a full head taller. I have no idea how this twelve-year-old-looking girl child thinks she's going to be served alcohol.

"Hey, so how about Truth or Dare?" she says, narrowing her eyes to slits.

"Here? In the cold like this?"

"You look like you can't feel anything right now."

This strikes me as hilarious.

"Okay. Dare," I say.

"Go and try to get that guy over there to go buy our liquor for us."

"That's bullshit. And so cliché. Is that the best dare you've got?"

"Okay," she says, leveling her little deep-set pixie eyes at me. "You're so brave? Go lay down on the double yellow lines in the middle of the road." As if to add drama to her dare, a van zips by her with a loud whine. Then another car.

"Ha. Your dares are weak," I say, and step into traffic. A big SUV blares his horn at me, swerves to avoid me, and zooms very close as he makes it by me. The road is dark in both directions, nothing but the liquor store light on about four house-lengths down. There is a streetlight by the liquor store, and another one about as far in the other direction, then the road curves and you can't see anything but trees and darkness. Another car swerves by me and beeps.

"Get out of the road, you idiot!" screams the driver.

I reach the double yellow lines. Sit down.

Quinn is still standing by the side of the road.

"Okay, you made your point," yells Quinn. "That guy's right.

You're an idiot. Get up!"

I feel another car zoom by me, fast, a blur of blue. I put my head down on the road. I am now straight on my back, parallel to the double yellow lines. They are narrower than I am.

"That's enough! You won Truth or Dare! Get up now," says Quinn, louder.

Another car rustles by me and I feel cold air on me. This could be the last second. This. Could. Be. It. It feels like a new idea, a revelation that has just occurred to me. More than that: I kind of wish it would be It.

I could end it here.

"Get up! You're so stupid! Come on!" Quinn sounds really frantic now. "Stop!"

I close my eyes. Zoom. Zoom. That last one felt so close. Thrilling. Right.

Suddenly I feel a hand on my wrist, pulling me up. It's Quinn. She's like five feet tall, but she pulls me up and drags me to the other side of the road. A minivan honks at us and honks as it drives away, its sound reproachful as it gets farther away. I look at Quinn and see that she is crying, her old little mouth scrunched up.

"You're so stupid, you know that? You were always a crazy little freak. Ever since kindergarten."

"You dared me."

"Those cars missed you by like a foot." She's really crying now.

"Calm down," I tell her. "They're never going to sell you booze if you look like a blotchy leprechaun."

"Short jokes. How original. Fine. Wait here." She wipes her face with the backs of her forearms and goes inside. I sit on the little raised bumps in one of the parking spots. She comes out with two bags that look way too heavy for her to carry. She drops one on my lap and it almost crashes to the ground.

"You gotta acknowledge Frank and Leslie for the genius of naming their kids so you can't tell whether we're boys or girls," she says, as if to herself.

"Genius."

"Shut up. I'm not even talking to you. I can't believe you pulled that shit in the road."

"You *dared* me."

"It's a miracle the human race has survived at all. You idiots with death wishes only think of yourselves."

I have a hard time keeping up as she takes a different way back to her house.

I go inside, leave the bag on her kitchen counter. Her kitchen is older, not marble perfection or stainless-steel modern chic. It's got a faintly dusty, somewhat abandoned look about it, a couple of small appliances I can't identify.

I walk into the dining room and see Patricia. No Jason.

"What's up?" I ask her. She looks like she's been crying.

"Nothing," she says.

"Not good?"

"Guys are jerks."

"Why don't we go to the bathroom and wash your face?"

She gets up, and I walk down a hallway, looking for a bathroom. I see a family portrait, Quinn little, even smaller than I remember her being in kindergarten, with four boys, all with the same flaming red hair and almost identical faces. It seems like they got it from their mother, a big, squarish woman with smiling eyes but the same old mouth.

"Which one is Grady, do you know?"

"I think that one," she says, pointing to the two-sizes-bigger-than-Quinn boy. "It's so sad about him, right?"

"What do you mean?"

"He killed himself. You must have heard."

"No. When?"

"Like a year ago."

"How?"

"Their mother's gun," she says.

I think of Quinn's voice, "*It's a miracle the human race has survived at all,*" and the way she started to cry. "I didn't know," I say.

My phone vibrates. I stare at it. When I see Nate's name on my caller ID, my heart thumps hard. I have cried about twenty times in the last three days about this. Nothing on Christmas Day. Nothing the day after that, or the day after that. And all those days, festering about Naomi. What he did with her. What he didn't tell me. What he may still be doing with her.

I finally pick up.

"Hello." I am pretty proud that I can pull off making "hello" sound like an accusation.

"Hey, M, how's it going?"

"Like you care."

"What do you mean? Are you okay?"

"Yes, I'm fine."

"I've missed you."

"Mmmm-hmmm."

"Why are you acting this way? Are you busy or something?"

He sounds so casual, like he's been fine.

"Yeah, I was on my way out, actually," I lie.

"Oh, because I'm back from my grandmother's and I thought maybe you might want to hang out."

"I didn't realize your grandmother lived on the moon."

"My grandma in Minnesota? My dad's mom? We just landed this morning."

"Yeah, but were you, like, in the Witness Protection Program while you were out there? Not a single phone call? Nothing?"

"I sent you a text when I first got there. Did you not get that?"

"Don't make up stupid stuff."

"I'm not. Why would I? I texted you when I got there and then my phone died."

"Really? You're going with the whole 'my phone died' thing?"

"What? Why would I lie about that?"

"When is Naomi's birthday?"

"What?"

"Your supposedly *ex*-girlfriend Naomi. When is her birthday?"

"Why is this—"

"*When?*"

"It was like a month ago. But what does this—"

"Did you see her?"

"No."

"No?"

"Listen, I don't want to keep repeating—"

"But you posted on her Facebook wall."

"There is a difference between seeing someone and posting on their wall. Although we go to school together, so it's possible I may have seen her walking around or something . . ."

"That's not really an answer."

"Was there a question?" Now he is sounding mad.

"The question was: did you post on her Facebook wall?"

"The answer is yes, I did post 'Happy Birthday' on her Facebook wall."

"You actually posted 'Happy Birthday, *rock star*' on her Facebook wall."

"She likes to sing. And anyway, what is the big deal?"

"The big deal is why did you break up?"

"I really don't think that's any of your business."

Now I'm furious. "What? You're really going to say that to me?"

"I think you need to calm down."

"I don't understand why you're hiding things from me."

"I'm not hiding anything from you. I just don't want to talk about this *this* way. Why don't I go pick you up and—"

"*No!* I don't want you to come pick me up. If I'm not important enough to know why the two of you broke up, and you obviously still have a thing for her and if she hadn't done what she did you'd still be with her."

"Wait. What? Can we start over? Because you're being the stereotypical crazy girlfriend right now."

The things that pop into my mind to say are way too mean, so

I hang up. My heart is pounding, my hands are shaking, and I am stunned that he got so cold and icy when I asked him questions.

All that needing someone ever does is give them the power to hurt you.

CHAPTER NINETEEN

Mr. Not-Ms. North has black hair and ginormous, black, bushy eyebrows and lips that look like they've been painted on. He is in a checkered button-down shirt and corduroy pants pulled up way too high. As soon as he opens his mouth, I decide I'm going to hate him.

"Welcome, class. I am your new professor," he says in an accent I can't place or completely understand. It sounds a little like Nate's Universal Accent. Nate. Argh. The thought of him makes a little ooze of sadness spread across my chest.

Mr. Not-Ms. North is still talking. "I have written my name on the board. It is pronounced Abedifirouzjaie." He says it the way it is spelled, which is to say, indecipherably. "Say it with me, please."

I scoot a little lower in my chair. A couple of people mumble something like "Abedifiblblb . . ."

"So, it is my understanding that you last read *The Winter's Tale*, is that correct?"

Ever-helpful Quinn says, "We were assigned to read *Othello* over break."

"Ah, yes, good, the Moor's tale. Of special significance to me. A fine play."

I am not sticking around for this. I don't want to stick around for anything. Ever.

I raise my my hand.

"Yes, young lady? And you have read the *Othello*, yes?"

"I have read the *Othello*, yes. I need to go to the office." I figure if I say it with enough authority, he'll think it's just a normal part of the routine.

"Ummm . . . this is . . . yes, you may go."

I take all my books and make sure to leave nothing. I'm done. Done. The plan is never to go back to that class.

I run down the stairs, down to the senior locker room. I sprawl across a bench, and don't even realize when I fall asleep.

When I wake up, I check the time: 1:15. I have soccer practice after school. The thought of it makes me want to fall back asleep. I realize there is no more point to soccer either. I walk over to the gym to find Coach Woods. I find her by the supply closet.

"Ms. Woods?"

"M.T., why aren't you in class?"

"I'm not feeling well. The nurse. Anyway, I wanted to talk to you about the team."

"What about it?"

"I'm . . . I think I need to quit."

"Quit? Why? What am I supposed to do for a forward?"

"I have to concentrate on my grades." Lie after lie starts to blur together, leaving me numb to them.

"That's never been a problem for you before."

"I know, but it is now."

"Look, I know it's important to concentrate on schoolwork. Why don't you skip practice today and then come to my office tomorrow and let's talk about some options?"

"Okay," I say. Even as I say it I know I will never go talk to her. I will stop going and eventually she'll just have to get it. I am perversely happy to cut one more little string holding me.

I figure it's late enough that anyone seeing me walking in the street will think I'm a student who got out early. I go back to my locker, put all my books in it, and leave. It feels strange to be out in the street before anyone else I know. I want to go somewhere, but I can't think of any place.

Chelsea gave me her old laptop during Christmas break, after she got a new one plus an iPad. It's opened up a few more options. I can check email at the coffee shop on the strip. They have Wi-Fi. I bike down there and sit in the corner farthest from the door. I fire up the laptop and get online.

There is new mail from Josh on Facebook. Every week, he's

been sending me obscure songs. Today's is "Blackberry Brandy" by T-Bird and the Breaks. Serious hillbilly music.

As I'm playing it, up pops a message from Josh.

"Did you like the song?"

I write back. "No." Is it weird to write to Chelsea's cousin's boyfriend?

"Well, that's good, Puff. It's like medicine. You're not supposed to like it."

"You're weird." I add, "What are you up to?"

"Actually, I'm coming down to your little neck of the Jersey Shore in a few weeks."

Hmmm. "I'm nowhere near the Jersey Shore. Why are you coming down?"

"I'm coming down to interview at Chelsea's mom's firm. I'll have to have my chest waxed and get a fake tan to blend in with the natives."

"I thought you'd be above stereotypes."

"True, true. You and Chelsea seem eminently reasonable. Even if you are from New Jersey."

"I guess."

"What about you? What are you doing this summer?"

"Nothing."

"Your enthusiasm is contagious."

"I don't know what I'm going to do next." I mean, it's true, but I don't know why he'd care.

"You should come up to Worthington. This would be a good school for you."

"I guess. I don't know." I am so tired of this senior year crap. Of people being oblivious.

"You sound pretty gloomy today. I have just the song for that. A classic. Painfully underrated." He sends a link. It comes over. "17 Ways to Say I'm Leaving."

I put in my headphones and listen. It's about a girl who is finding ways to say good-bye to all the people in her life before she takes an overdose. Seventeen ways. *"I'm sorry I left you. I had no choice."* I close my eyes and let the eerie violin play over me. It says something to me I've never heard before but which sounds weirdly like coming home. Like finding answers. The refrain is the girl singing, then a little chorus of kids echoing what she says. Creepy and sad. It's like it turns a light bulb on in my head.

I have racked my brain for a way out, for solutions.

Treading water. Trying to keep from going under. Exhausted. I just want some rest.

This song finally makes it feel so simple. I can't believe it's never occurred to me until now. I can make it all stop. Take action. I can finally have peace. No more smacks. No more empty future.

No more friends leaving. No more everyone leaving—Chelsea, Nate, Ms. North, my parents in the immigration van. No more Jose crying. No more fatherless Julissa with the dirty linoleum in her mouth. No more anyone leaving. All I have to do is be the one to leave.

Nothing anymore. No more being afraid or tired or ashamed.

People always talk about fighting being the brave thing. But maybe the bravest thing is knowing when to stop. Knowing when you are beat. It is such a simple answer. It almost makes me happy.

Here are all the things you gave me. Here are all the blows and lies. Here are the tales you told me. This is why I say good-bye.

I play the song in a loop over and over again. It is the first time in a long time I have felt someone has been pointing to the answer. The nun's devil is sitting on my shoulder, whispering in my ear. I get up and go to the drugstore. I need a razor blade. It's what I've always needed.

I GET HOME AFTER DARK. NO ONE IS AWAKE.

Jose is in bed. I unfold the futon and get into it.

"You're home so late," he says.

"I'm sorry I woke you, little dude."

"I wasn't sleeping."

With the little snores I heard, I beg to differ, but you never call Jose on having been asleep. As far as he's concerned, he never sleeps.

"All right, well, you should go to sleep then. You have school tomorrow."

"You too."

Well, questionable. Haven't decided.

"Monse? What do people do after they finish high school?"

"They usually go to college. Or they can get a job."

"Which one are you going to do?"

"I haven't decided yet."

"Are you going to leave?"

"Sometimes colleges are like sleepaways."

He starts to cry. "You can't leave me."

It does suck to think of leaving him with these two.

"Don't worry, there's a long time until that happens. Like months."

"Are you going to move away?"

There is one person I've never told a lie to, and that's this kid. I should just say no and he'll fall asleep. But then one day I won't be here anymore, and he'll know I lied.

"Yes. One day I won't live here anymore."

He starts to cry harder.

"Who will watch *SpongeBob* with me?"

"One day you won't want to watch *SpongeBob* anymore and it won't matter. Please don't worry about it now."

"I'll give you all my clothes so you can remember me by."

Now I want to cry. Plus if there's one thing I don't want to remember him by, it's his ugly hand-me-downs. "Come over here," I say.

He climbs out of his bed and onto my futon. I feel his warm, bony back nestle against me. I run the back of my fingers on his tears. "You know, if one day I'm not here, it's not because I don't want to be with you."

"Can I come with you?"

"No, silly."

"But why?"

I don't know what answer to give him. So I say, "Let's fall asleep."

"Okay."

It takes him a long time to finally fall asleep. He's like me that way. But he's little, so I can outlast him. When he's out, I pick him up and put him back in his bed, SpongeBob pillow under his arm the way he likes it. He is so beautiful.

I reach into my backpack for the drugstore bag. I fish around in the dark for my package. I go in the kitchen and fumble around for the candles and matches my mom keeps in there for when our electricity gets disconnected.

I go into the bathroom, close the door, fire up the laptop, and listen to the song with my headphones on. I hide the razor blade. Just knowing it's there makes me feel brave.

On Saturday, I drag my feet to the kitchen and my mother is there, dressed and looking like she's going to go out.

"Oh, good, you're awake." She smiles at me.

"Mmmm."

"I'm glad, because I need you to sit with Jose for a few hours," she says. She is way too chipper.

What about your husband? I want to ask.

"And where are you going?" my father says, coming out of his room.

"My class starts on Tuesday, so I need to go buy some notebooks and pencils and things." Is *that* what she's so happy about? What an idiot. *Yeah, go learn some English so you'll understand what they're saying to you when they deport you.* "Also, Mrs. Nussbaum wants new curtains, so I'm going to go measure."

"New curtains, huh? And who's going to be teaching this class?"

"I'm not sure. It's at the library."

"You know the library is a public thing, right? That it's run by the government? What kinds of papers did they ask you for to sign up?" he asks.

"No, nothing, they said it was . . ." She trails off, looking worried.

"They said it was what?"

"They said it was open to anyone. No requirements or anything."

"Oh, yeah? Is that what they told you?"

"The Nun suggested it. I mean, she must know because—"

"You think The Nun cares about you? You go to your class and you see what's going to happen to you."

"Jorge, what do you think is going to happen?" She looks really scared.

"I'm just saying you go on Tuesday and you'll see. This is not going to end well."

"I just want to learn English."

"Okay, you go learn English. Just say good-bye to your children before you go."

My mother still leaves, but with a lot less bounce in her step.

Score 1 for the Grim Sleeper.

Well, more like score 1,300,000.

NATE CALLS AGAIN IN THE AFTERNOON. I DON'T KNOW IF WE'RE broken up or what. It feels like we are.

"Can I please see you?" he says. And because I'm tired of everything, including being mad and scared, I say yes.

I don't bother to do the whole dolling up thing. I wait ten minutes, then go wait for him outside in my sweatpants and hair in a ponytail. I probably don't smell great. But there is no point washing up for the end.

He kisses my cheek. "Are you still mad at me?"

"Why didn't you call me for all those days?" I had told myself I would play it cool, but it falls out of my mouth before I can stop myself. The online advice gurus would not approve.

"When I was at my grandma's, you mean?"

"Yeah, Christmas. After Christmas."

"I called you as soon as I got home."

"But while you were there?"

"She lives in Podunk somewhere. No wireless, terrible reception. And I forgot my charger like a dumb-ass. Plus my cousins were all there . . . I mean, I don't know, M. I thought you understood I was going away."

I say nothing. I am not going to make him understand. And

now, the anger fading, I'm not sure I know how to explain.

"Hey, can I ask you? What was that Naomi thing?" he asks.

"I saw that she Liked your picture with your cousins, so that made me go on her profile. It felt bad. It felt terrible, actually."

"What did?"

"To see pictures of the two of you together. To know that—"

"That was, like, last summer."

"Why are you still posting on her Wall?"

"Because we go to school together. Because we're friends. It's no big deal. Because Facebook pops up those little reminders on the right side of the page and you don't even have to click through to write something."

"I know what Facebook does."

"I just wanted to be a nice guy and wish her a happy birthday. Is that really that bad?"

"Did she break your heart?"

"The cheating thing?"

"Yeah."

"It's so crazy how much people talk. Honestly, we were kind of already not seeing each other. She wasn't that into having a boyfriend. And I . . . I don't know. It was kind of boring."

"Like with me?"

"This is a totally different thing."

"Is there an N and N ankle bracelet floating around some-where?"

He puts his arm around me.

"Nope."

"It sort of bothers me that you guys share a first initial."

He laughs. "Should I change my name? Maybe I can be one of those guys who spells his name backward."

"Etan."

"Not bad. Too close to Ethan, though. We'd need it to be really freaky. Maybe use my full name. Leinahtan."

"Sounds vaguely Hawaiian."

"We could move to Molokai and I could wear a sarong all day," he jokes, kissing my cheek, near my lips.

I stare at the floor of his car. I don't understand how he so easily survives for days like that without me, when I feel like the color has drained out of the world when I'm without him.

He says, "I'm sorry I hurt you. I didn't realize I was doing that."

I move my face and kiss him. At least he's here now.

CHAPTER TWENTY

"M.T., did you hear me?"

I look up from my doodle to see a very creased-looking Ms. Kracowitz, staring at me.

"I'm sorry, what was that, Ms. Kracowitz?"

"I said I don't see your homework here."

"Oh. I guess I don't have it." Since after Christmas break, I've sort of stopped doing most of it.

"I'd like to speak to you after class."

I shuffle my feet up to the front of the class.

"Yes, Ms. Kracowitz?"

"This is the first year I've had you in class, and, to be honest, I haven't been impressed. But I'm assured by other teachers that you are a very dedicated student and your past grades and test scores would seem to indicate that. So I'm confused. Are you not understanding the material?"

I consider telling her I have not read any of the textbook or paid attention for weeks, but I'm not sure that's going to help this conversation along.

THE SECRET SIDE OF EMPTY

"I guess some of it is hard."

"You know I'm here every Tuesday and Thursday after school for extra help?"

"Yes."

"I haven't seen you once this year."

Would "no" sound rude here?

"Listen, M.T., I understand that one gets itchy at the end of senior year. It happened to me. It happens to a lot of us. You're eager for what comes next."

Well, not exactly.

"But you've got to make it out of high school first. You just have to make it through a few months and then you'll have the whole summer to relax before you go off to school and start a bright new future." She is warming up to her own pep talk, puffing up with pleasure at how cool she is, acknowledging that senior year is boring and pointless. I wonder if she'll sit in the teachers' lounge later, telling the other teachers, "I had one of those lazy seniors stay after class, and I gave her the 'the world is your oyster' speech. And that fixed everything." *Good for you, Ms. Kracowitz. Good for you.*

"Ms. Kracowitz. Can I ask you something?"

"Yes?"

"You knew Ms. North?" It's a small school, and there aren't that many of them, so she must have.

"Yes, Cathy. Sure." It always creeps me out to hear teachers referring to each other by their first names. It creeps me out to think teachers *have* first names.

"Have you heard from her since she left?"

"We met for coffee just last weekend. She is in a new, more senior position. She's very happy."

I want to ask if she's asked about me, but it sounds ridiculous in my head, so I don't.

"You know, I'm sure she'd love to hear from you. She gave you all her email address before she left, right?"

"Yes." I don't mention that I crumpled the sheet up into a million little pieces in the locker room garbage can.

"Well, okay, then. Get to your next class."

"Okay."

"And I'll see you Tuesday after school."

No, you won't.

On the way down the hall, Patricia stops me.

"Hey, M, Mackenzie says she's tried to call you for tutoring, like, three times but she can't seem to get in touch with you."

I'm kinda not tutoring the way I'm kinda not studying. It feels weirdly good to let it all go, one thing at a time.

I don't say this. I say, "Oh, yeah? I have so many tutoring customers." Lie. I am getting better at this.

"But you'll get back to Mack, right? She's, like, totally flunking math and she won't let me help her. She says just you."

"I guess. I'll see."

I don't want to tutor. I don't want to not tutor. I want to fall asleep and be at rest. Find my way to say good-bye to this whole stupid mess.

NATE AND I ARE SITTING BY THE KITCHEN ISLAND WHEN HIS mother blows by with her usual cloud of activity around her.

"Honey, I'm off to go shopping because I can't find a single thing to wear to your father's awards thing tomorrow night. And Carmen picked up your suit from the dry cleaner's. It's on your valet rack. For God's sake pick out a tie that doesn't have cartoon characters on it. And Jackson will probably get here when I'm not here. Tell him Carmen has made up the downstairs guest room for him."

"'K, Mom."

And then she's gone.

"What's that all about? Suit?"

"My father has some lame dinner where they're giving him some award. We all have to go."

"Jackson?"

"Becky's boyfriend."

"He's going?"

"Yeah, and Emily is coming from school."

"With *her* boyfriend?"

"Yeah."

My heart starts thumping, waiting for him to put two and two together. Anger rising fast.

"When were you planning on telling me this?" I ask. We usually spend Friday nights together.

"My mom told me, like, weeks ago, but I totally forgot until she started in with the suit thing yesterday."

"And Jackson is going?"

"I just said that."

"But I'm not invited."

"M, you're not going to make this a thing, are you?"

I am learning that him not understanding why I'm mad makes me even madder than what I'm originally mad about.

"It doesn't occur to you that it might feel crappy to be the one girlfriend . . . boyfriend . . . whatever . . . that is not invited?"

"It's not like that. They get a table. There are a certain number of chairs at the table. I don't get to decide who goes. It's us and some people from my dad's office."

"Did you bother to ask?"

"It didn't even occur to me. These things are so boring, I wish

I could get out of going. Why would I drag you to that?"

"Because it might be a nice way of showing people that we're the real deal? That you're not ashamed of me?"

"I'm not ashamed . . . what? You're over my house like *every day*. Why would I be—"

"I just don't get how everyone is going, everyone is bringing boyfriends, but you don't think of me enough to think that maybe this is the kind of thing I should be at?"

"Honestly, M, I don't know what to say to you when you get like this."

"Forget it."

Right in that moment, Emily walks in. If she feels the tension in the room, she ignores it. But more likely she is just too carried along in the puff of happiness that floats around with her all the time, the my-life-is-so-perfect-I-don't-really-need-any-good-reason-to-be-happy" puff.

She hangs up her coat in the coat closet but leaves her scarf and a beret on.

As she gets closer, I notice that her skin is so flawless it seems painted on. I try to narrow my eyes to see if that's foundation. She's a freaking CoverGirl commercial. I want to like Emily, but people who are straight-up nice like her make me feel like I am being made fun of somehow.

"Hey, so where is everyone?" she asks.

"Shopping. Otherwise engaged," says Nate.

"I was thinking of heading to the mall, too. I need something to wear to Dad's thing tomorrow. Do you guys want to come?"

For some bizarre reason, I really want to go to the mall with Emily. Or just get out of here.

"Nate, let's go," I say.

"Ummm . . . the mall and dresses. I don't think so." He still looks pretty pissed off at me.

"Come on!" says Emily.

"Why don't you go with Emily?" he asks me.

It hadn't occurred to me. I look at her, looking for signs of "ewww." I just get that CoverGirl smile back. "You wanna?" she says.

"Sure." Perhaps I will uncover the source of the giant scarves.

"We'll have dinner at the mall and then swing by to pick you up for a movie. Cool, Natey?" she asks. She actually ruffles his hair.

The dinner and movie thing sets off an alarm for me because I have only ten dollars in my pocket. Ten stolen dollars at that.

We jump into one of the cars in the driveway. I wonder if she just picks at random or if this one is hers. She starts it and says to me, "It's so good to see him. Even though I'm at school right in the city, I feel like I hardly see them now. That's why I come home so much. I miss my family a lot."

I wonder what that feels like. Not being sure you have to escape.

We get to the mall and she heads to Nordstrom. She tries on boot after boot—despite the fact that I thought we were on a dress-finding mission—chattering all the while about her life in New York, her classes, her boyfriend. She settles on three pairs and heads over to the Gap. I discover the source of the giant scarves. She drapes a cream-colored one on me.

"M, that looks amazing on you. It works so well with your coloring."

Hmmm. It does look kind of nice. I take it off. The label scratches my ear. I hold it in my hands and look at it. Then I put it back.

She walks up the aisles getting random stuff—a backpack, some shoes, a bunch of scarves. I walk over to the jeans and look while she does her thing. She walks up to me with a bunch of bags in her hands.

"You ready?" she says.

"Yeah."

Outside the Gap, she hands me a bag. "Here," she says. "Let's go to dinner now." I peek inside. The scarf. I want the scarf just enough to not say no to her. But it's heavy in my hands, too, the way all charity feels, like it takes away some little thing in you that's worth something. I hate when people give me things, but I especially hate how much I want them to.

We're halfway through the pot stickers at the mall restaurant when she says, "So how are you and Natey going to keep it together with him gone all summer? Have you guys talked about it?"

My heart starts pounding. I don't know what she's talking about, but I don't want to let on. "Yeah, well, you know, what can you do?" Vague enough to go with anything.

"I was, like, 'Nate, a whole summer working as a deckhand on a boat?' What kind of thing is that? He says it's not a deckhand, but they definitely have to work. The last summer before you go away to college you're supposed to relax, you know?" I flash back to that conversation in the car when we wished about weird jobs. Did he joke about being a deckhand? I try to remember.

I want to run into the parking lot and scream. I press my earlobe where the tag scratched me earlier. It stings. I focus on that and say, "Yeah, but it's what he wants to do."

"You're such an understanding girlfriend," she says, with the tone you'd use when you're saying, "What a cute puppy."

I sit numb all through dinner, my giant scarf making my neck itchy. Nate is already gone like I always knew he would be.

CHAPTER TWENTY-ONE

The air is warming and Goretti is abuzz with the Europe trip. Since Ms. North left, I have stopped helping organize. I am happy about that for a lot of reasons, but mostly because Ms. Cronell has taken over as NHS moderator. Every insufferable NHS meeting begins and ends with Europe details. The hotel in Ireland went out of business, says the tour company. They need to pick a new one. Did everyone bring in copies of their passports? Dakota has helpfully drafted a travel checklist. It includes such key things like, "Pack hair spray," and "Make photocopies of everything in your wallet."

I want to set fire to the whole stack.

At the end of the meeting, Ms. Cronell asks me to help her carry some things to the teachers' lounge. Everyone else walks away, and Ms. Cronell puts down the things she's carrying.

"Monserrat, I need to speak to you about something." The way she says my name, she makes it sound like a curse word somehow.

She wants to talk. Oh boy. Not good.

"It has been brought to my attention by several teachers that your grades are slipping."

It's not a question, so I don't feel the need to say anything.

"You understand that in order to remain in the NHS, you must maintain a certain grade point average. And a certain attitude."

Stare. I notice three unruly chin hairs that move up and down when she talks.

"You've also had an unusual number of absences this year."

Stare. Those chin hairs are positively dancing.

"I hope you don't think you're somehow above the rules. NHS vice president or no, if your grades fall below the expected average, you will be removed from the group. Do you understand?"

It is obvious she's not getting the please-don't-kick-me-out-of-the-NHS reaction she would expect from the super-geek I used to be. She is expecting hysterics, or at least crying. Begging. Maybe bribery? Lord knows she could do with some new wardrobe money.

"Do you understand what I'm saying to you? I'm talking about having to return your pin. Not being able to wear the NHS sash at graduation."

I have to hold in a laugh. She looks at me strangely while my eyes get wide and I twist up my face to hold the laugh back. A pin? A sash? *Seriously*?

"If you don't bring up your grades immediately, you will be removed from the National Honor Society roster. And it will go on your permanent record."

Stare. *Oh, please, anything but that.* I wish I had a tweezer for those chin hairs.

"That won't look good for colleges. Don't think that because it's the end of senior year, they won't take notice." She stops, looks all over my face. "Can you say something, please? Do you understand? Don't you think you can hold it together for just a few months more?" She searches my face for a reaction. I see her face almost soften for a split second. I haven't said anything to her little scare speech. I focus on the chin hairs. One is gray, two are black.

Finally, I say, "I don't know, Ms. Cronell. But I don't think so."

"I'll have to bring this to the attention of your parents."

Silence.

She nods, just down once, not up. I guess she gets it.

I think this merits a day off. I go out through the locker room door so no one sees me leave.

I CAN'T THINK OF ANYWHERE TO GO. I RIDE TO THE APARTMENT. The stairs feel so long and exhausting. I go into my room and drop on the futon.

My eyes feel like they're sinking into my head. I close them, trying to force myself to fall asleep. I stay in that position for a long time, the light in the room changing, dimming, until it's gone. I drift off at some point. When I wake up, my head feels achy, like there is a hollow in my forehead that is filled with gray fog.

I go to the bathroom. I feel under the sink. There it is. The razor blade. My escape hatch. My ticket. Not today but one day maybe. *As the rivers run dry, making up my mind.*

For now, I stare at my face. What a big nose. My skin is a mess. I am pale, and I have big circles under my eyes. No wonder Nate wants to go away and not be near me. No wonder I don't belong here. I wash my face, hoping the cold water will make me feel better. It doesn't. I root around the medicine cabinet and find an old jar of face cream I used to see my mother use. When I uncap it, it has a brown crust around the rim. The cream looks fine, though. I slather it on my face, and it feels like it has ice in it, something minty. I let it sit. Then I wipe it off, and wash the last of it off with cold water. I still feel exhausted, but awake.

I look around at my mother's makeup. She's got some garish red lipstick that I've never seen her wear. I uncap it, look at it, run it across my bottom lip. It is shocking against my pasty skin. I like how this makes me look like someone else.

I am looking at myself in the mirror this way when the door slams open. The old brass hook on the back of the door rattles to the floor.

"What the hell are you doing in here?" asks my father. I hadn't even known he was home.

"Nothing."

"Didn't you hear me telling you I need to get in here?"

"No." Truth.

His eyes focus on the makeup. "Why are you putting that crap on?"

"I'm just . . . I don't know . . . I was just . . ."

He grabs a fistful of my hair and slams my face into the mirror, pinning the lipstick between me and the mirror. I feel the lipstick slither up my face, smushing against the mirror.

"Don't think I don't know what you're up to. Your lies. I am totally sick of your disrespect. You think you're so smart, ignoring me, making me wait for the bathroom? You are good for nothing, you know that?" He emphasizes his statements with a little press into the mirror, and I start to worry what will happen if the mirror breaks.

"Leave me alone!"

"Stop lying. I know you. I see right through you. You think you're so smart. You're just like I was at your age. Just wait until life teaches you a thing or two."

That's the worst insult of all, him thinking I'm like him at all.

"Get off me!" I scream.

"Or what?"

"Just get off me. What is your problem?"

"What is my problem?" He laughs, a dark, angry little sound. "I have a lot of problems," he says, giving my face one last shove into the mirror. "Get the hell out of the bathroom. I told you I need to use it."

I hate my eyeballs for betraying me with tears. I can't let him see. I won't give him that satisfaction. I grab some toilet paper and rub the red mark off my face and my lips. I wash with soap as fast as I can, then run in my room and grab a bag. I am done. I am leaving. Jeans. Underwear. As many shirts as will fit. My phone. My charger. A handful of pictures. Emily's big scarf. No, not that, it takes up too much room. I drape it around my neck, although it's getting a little warm for that. Rumi's poems that Ms. North gave me. Not much else fits, so this will have to be enough, until I figure out where I'm going.

I ride and ride, opposite the way I normally go. I ride in the direction of the big park, not Nate and mine's. I'm thinking of that little field house. Maybe the lock will be flimsy and I can sleep in there. If not, it's not that cold. I'll find a little out-of-the-way spot in the park. It'll be fun. It will be like camping. And tomorrow I will figure out where I am going to go.

When I get to the field house, the lock is built into the metal door. Impossible to break in. I ride around, looking for some other open structure. Nothing. I am seriously unschooled in the art of being a hobo.

I pull out my phone. I ache to call someone. Chelsea. I could sleep over at Chelsea's and tell her everything and finally it would be okay. Or Nate.

But I can't. How would I explain anything that's going on in my life to them? It would sound so ridiculous, so impossible next to the lives they're living. Also, how do you explain to someone that you are so horrible and useless that your own father despises you? I am so ashamed. I don't want them to know because I know they'll figure out what that means about me. The dirty, ugly outcast I really am.

It's getting really dark and I find an old willow in a quiet spot behind the soccer field. I sit under it for hours, until I'm too sleepy to sit up. The moon is a little slit. It turns out it's a bunch colder at night. I put on the second pair of jeans over the ones I'm wearing, and a couple of the shirts, too. Then I put on my jacket over all that. Emily's scarf makes a pretty good pillow. It gets all kinds of dirty, though.

I curl up and try to fall asleep. For a while, I hear some voices in the distance, laughter, and then nothing. I bet serial killers laugh like that. Who knew the park was this creepy at night? There are critters and noises that just don't stop. I think the serial killers are getting closer.

I temporarily imagine building a little hut out of twigs. That sounds like so much work, though. Plus, the bugs. No way. I pull out my phone. Fifty percent charge. And it's only 11:52. That seals it. I can't do another seven hours of this.

I pick up my bike and start pedaling back home, slowly.

CHAPTER TWENTY-TWO

Mr. Abedifirouzjaie (or Mr. A, as he has mercifully allowed us to call him) tells me during lunchtime that he'd like to see me after school. I have skipped his class as I do on most days, so I'm assuming he wants to have a little powwow about that. So I go.

"Monserrat. Thank you for coming." Strangely, his accent makes it so that he's got the best pronunciation of my name I've heard in a while.

"Hi."

"How are you finding my class?" he says.

I want to say, "I didn't know it was lost," but instead I say, "Good."

"Also optional, I notice."

"Ummm . . . this morning I had to go to the nurse . . ."

"Let's both spare ourselves the indignity of your story, shall we?"

"Okay."

"I thought perhaps you might be one of those with the . . . how do you say it here? Senior fever? But then I asked around and learned that you used to be quite an applied student."

Applied student? Is that like a glue brand or something?

"And then I did the further inquiries and discovered that you were a special student to Ms. North, my predecessor."

Stare. Say nothing.

"I must be quite a disappointment after your most beloved teacher leaves." The skin around his eyes squints a little and he looks like someone's grandfather, right at the moment when he's going to give a lollipop.

"I . . . no . . . it's just—"

"Look, we will never have what you and Ms. North had. Alas, we lack the time, and even if we did, there are some holes only one person can fill. Would you not say yes to this?"

His accent is goofy, but I am somehow starting to get it.

"I would say yes to that."

"Good. I am an old and strange man with what must seem to you a very silly accent. Is that the way of it?"

"Well, sometimes it's hard—"

"You know what it means when someone has an accent?" he asks, kindly, with a smile.

"That they were born—"

"It means that they speak one more language than you do. I myself speak five. And you?"

"Two. And a little Italian I guess."

"That's more than most. Although it would seem perhaps at least that you might have a few things to learn from me. Would you not say?"

"Yes."

"It may seem funny for someone who speaks English with an accent to be teaching the English. But what I like to say is that you can only truly love a place when you have lived outside it."

I think about the little things I've noticed, like how in Spanish there are two different kinds of "you," the formal one for teachers and cops and elders and the informal for friends and younger people. He actually has a point.

"Have you read any Nabokov?" he asks me.

"No."

"The ultimate example, I would say, of a nonnative speaker of English relishing the English language as only a nonnative can. Although do not let the nuns catch me recommending *Lolita* to you. Now we each have something on each other. I know you don't come to class. You know I recommend literature absolutely inappropriate for young girls to young girls."

"A mutual destruction pact." I smile.

He's quiet for a minute. "You only hurt yourself when you don't come to class."

I nod a little.

"I know the standard teacher thing to do is to call your parents, have the big conversation. This, I suspect, would not be of help with you."

"Why?" I'm curious.

"Other teachers have spoken to your mother."

"They have?"

"She's right in the building next door. How would they not? Here is what I propose. Please come to class now. I will bore you, but it will be more informative than napping in the senior locker room. Read what you like and I will not shame you in class too much when you don't know what I am talking about. You may even get enough information to do reasonably well on tests. Does this sound possible to you?"

"Maybe. Yes. I guess."

"A resounding agreement. One last thing. I will also be expecting the final Ms. North described to you. The world view position paper. That one thing is not negotiable. I will look the other way if you are less than motivated in class, but you must write that paper. Imagine you are writing it to present to her. Deal?"

"Deal."

NATE ASKED ME YESTERDAY IF WE COULD HANG OUT TODAY, AND although I've been avoiding him since Emily's little revelation, I say yes. I miss him so badly, but I'm afraid I don't have the energy to hold up the picture of me that he wants to see. I'm afraid to ask him about his summer plans because once I do that, they will be real.

When I get out of school, he's waiting. I get in. I want to lean over and kiss him but I feel too shy to do it. He feels far away.

He doesn't put the car in drive. He sits there, looking at the rearview mirror, like someone's chasing him. Then he studies his thumbnail.

"M, I don't know how to tell you this."

"What?"

"I . . . I don't think we should see each other anymore."

And there go the waterworks. I need to get a better hold on that.

"Please don't cry. I'm so sorry." He puts his hand on mine.

"What happened?" I ask. Ugh. Too needy. There are times when the thing you fear the most turns out to not feel as bad as you thought it would. This is not one of those times. It hurts more than anything, ever.

"It's just . . . I don't know. You seem so sad. I seem to hurt you so much, and I'm not sure how."

"*That's* not it," I say, loud, accusing. I think I blow some tears and snot on him. Not attractive. "It's just that you planned all along to sneak off and not tell me anything. How long did you know you were going on this boat thing?"

"M, why do you have to raise your voice? That's exactly what I'm talking about. Like you're always at the edge of exploding. I applied to the boat thing before I met you. It's something I've always wanted to do. But it's not that. You're always so sad or mad, like you're unhappy with me and you won't tell me why. I just feel so guilty around you all the time."

I feel desperate, like I have to find the right combination of words to stop this from happening. I am losing the best of me: him. I have to help him see that he's not the problem. I have to find the words to make him stay. "Why didn't you tell me about the summer thing?"

"I thought about it so many times. But it never seemed like the right time."

"If I'm such a mess, why did you stay with me at all? Why did you put up with me at all?" It feels so familiar, him deciding I'm not good enough for him. I've lived it so many times in my head that now that it's finally here, I recognize it like something that's already happened.

"I don't think you're a mess, M. I just don't think I'm the guy for you. I can't seem to . . . I don't know. You don't look happy when you're around me. I'm always making you mad."

"Please let's try again. I'm so sorry if I seemed mad. It wasn't you. It's just stuff at home. I'm so sorry." I'm slobbering big time on his shirt now, at his shoulder. He puts his arm around me, but he doesn't seem very enthusiastic about it.

"M, it's bound to happen anyway. I want to go to college not feeling like you're sitting at home waiting. I couldn't stand the thought of being away this summer and feeling you were home unhappy because I didn't call enough or something."

I sob and try to catch my breath on his shoulder. "It's just that I love you. So. Much." I say. That doesn't quite put into words the way I feel but it's all I can come up with.

He's quiet for a moment. "I know," he says. "And that's what scares me."

Nothing, anywhere, ever, will ever hurt as much as this moment.

I try to get out of the car, because it seems like that's what would happen in the movie version of this, but he holds my hand and says, "Let me take you home." He feels sorry for me. I put my face in my hands and sob the whole way home, hating myself for doing it. I want to explain to him that my world stops without him. I look inside my head for the words. I find none. His hand is on the knob that changes the car from park to reverse to drive. He grips it so tightly that the skin stretches around his knuckles.

He pulls up to my apartment building. I know the dignified thing would be to straighten up, wipe off my face, and say that I hope one day we will be friends. But I want to chain myself to the seat in his car so he has to take me with him. I can feel how uncomfortable he is, but this doesn't make me move.

Finally, he says, "Can we still go to your prom together?" I notice he doesn't mention his.

"I don't need your pity."

"It's not pity. It's that I promised you months ago and it's not fair to change things a month before."

"It's fine. Don't worry about it." I feel icky at his consolation prize.

"Honestly, I think it would be nice to go."

"Whatever. I don't care." It's the thought of the pity prom date that finally propels me out of the car.

CHAPTER TWENTY-THREE

He is near me. I'm on the grass on my back and he's propped on an elbow, smiling down at me, the sun a halo behind him. It makes me squint. This beautiful boy is my boyfriend. I am so lucky. It's so improbable. I look at the pattern of freckles on his nose, the sparkly green of his eyes.

Of course. *Of course.* I soak in the joy of him, the way his two front teeth are a little bigger than the others, the way his bottom lip is fuller than his top one, and that it reaches me a nanosecond sooner when he leans in to kiss me. His nose turns up and his eyelashes grow all the way to the very inside of his eyes in a way I've never seen anyone's eyelashes grow before.

Kiss me. I don't say it, but he senses it and leans in, his smile turning into a soft laugh, sexy, happy. Yes. Of course. It's perfect. Like a hammock on a warm day, safe. Like a stack of new books, chocolate mousse cake, swinging high on the swings. Like jumping off a branch and discovering you can glide. His shirt smells like cotton and detergent and sun.

He leans in closer. In the silence, the gap between the moments feels eternal.

"Just stay," I say.

"Of course I'm going to stay." I know he is going to kiss me and then he does it. My heart stops first, then speeds up.

But I've forgotten something. Like an item I've forgotten to put on a list. Towels. Sheets. A hair dryer. Band-Aids. What is it?

My eyes open. I am confused. Jerked into another time and place. Where?

My futon.

No sunshine.

What happened?

And then . . . of course. The thousand sinking wishes. The color bleeding out of everything. Of course. He isn't really going to kiss me. My mind thinks it helps by bringing him to me in my sleep.

He isn't ever going to kiss me again. I can't think of anything sadder. I've just played the cruelest trick on myself, cracked some little thing inside. To lift up my hopes just to have to lose him all over again hurts just as much as the first time. It is raw and fresh and real, like he's just now said the words again: "I don't think we should see each other anymore." The loss I feel is bottomless, like I can never get any more alone than right now.

Anticipating it a thousand times didn't prepare me. It only made it worse.

CHAPTER TWENTY-FOUR

I am getting used to not going to school. I keep my deal with Mr. A only some of the time. Some days I go for attendance and his class, then hang around inside. I stare off blankly in classes in which teachers take attendance, and nap in the locker room through those where teachers don't. I haven't been to gym in weeks, and no one seems to have noticed.

Other days, I leave the house but don't go at all. A few times, when I've had stolen cash, I've taken the bus into the city and walked around all day until it's time to go home. Today I don't have the energy. Or the cash. I go sit in the bushes outside the library. Fire up the laptop. Facebook. Gossip sites. Email. Nothing, nothing, nothing. I am not sure how I am going to do five more hours of this.

And then I hear steps. Really close. I look up and there's a cop.

He says, "I'm going to need you to get out of the bushes now. And let me see your hands."

So this is how it ends. After all the years of being afraid of it, knowing it's here is terrifying but also weirdly calming, like at least

I finally know. He's going to ask for papers, he's going to find out I have none, and I am done. On a plane to Argentina tonight. How could I have been so stupid?

"Is there a problem, Officer?"

"Yeah, the problem is that you're hiding in the bushes when you should be in school. How old are you?"

"Nineteen."

"Lying to me isn't really a good idea right now. How old are you really?"

Is lying to him an offense that could get me arrested? Or am I in trouble regardless?

"Look, I'm going to be calling your family and your school, so we can do this the easy way or we can do this the hard way."

"Seventeen. I'm a senior."

"You're not done yet with school then, are you?"

"What if I told you I'm a dropout?"

"The way you asked me, I can tell you're not. Let me see some ID."

ID. *Thud, thud, thud.* My pulse is in my ears and I feel nauseous. He's going to run me against some national database and I am going to be outed. I am already outed, maybe. Things look far away, like I'm looking at them through a tube. I try to suck in a breath so I won't pass out.

I guess he can tell because he says, "Listen, relax. Walk over to the station with me."

"Am I arrested?"

"I told you, I'm just calling your mother."

"She's working."

"She's getting called anyway. Or would you rather I called your father?" I guess the answer to that is usually no because he smiles a little when he says it.

"He's in the city."

"Let's go, then. Let me see your license."

"I don't drive." He looks at me funny. "Really, I mean it. I haven't taken the test."

He cocks his head like he's trying to figure out whether that's true.

"Your school ID then."

That I do have. But it's got my real name and everything. I curse myself for not getting some kind of fake ID for these situations. I fumble in my backpack and hand it over.

"Goretti, huh? Didn't the nuns teach you more sense than to cut school when you're almost finished?"

I'm not sure if he's really expecting an answer to that, so I say nothing. I can't believe it all ends like this. It's all in slo-mo.

I wonder if I could outrun this guy. He seems a little out of shape. I should have stuck with the dropout story. But I just crumbled. I think of Baby Julissa with her dad in a van, off to jail, and then who knows where else. My mother. Jose.

I alternate between wild hope that somehow he'll let me go, followed by the sinking feeling of knowing this is how I get busted. I am done here. Done.

The door of the municipal complex slides open noiselessly and I'm hit by a frigid wall of air. We walk past a big glass window like you'd see in a bank. There is another cop behind it.

He says, "Hey, Charlie."

"Joe."

"Whatcha got there?"

"A Goretti girl."

Charlie chuckles. "No kidding," he says, and moves his hand along the wall. A buzzer sounds. The cop called Joe opens a big metal door and lets me step through first.

"Okay, come this way," he says.

I wonder how this whole thing will work. If I'll get to see my parents before they send me back. Or if they'll send us all back and it's my fault that Jose will have to go back with them.

Cop Joe walks me over to a desk and points to a chair alongside it.

"Here, sit down."

I do and hug my backpack to my chest.

"You got anything in that bag I should know about?"

I shake my head.

"I'm going to need to take a look inside. You okay with that?"

For a second I consider asking him if I'm under arrest and if he has a warrant or probable cause. All the cop show stuff. But I hand him my backpack.

He opens it up. It's empty except for the laptop. And a few loose tampons at the bottom. He opens the front pocket, but doesn't look too carefully.

"Traveling kind of light these days, huh?"

"I guess."

"Getting ready to graduate?"

"Yeah."

"You're not going to make it if you keep cutting school."

"I know."

"Anything you want to tell me about? Any problems?"

"No."

"So what are you doing?"

He actually doesn't look that menacing. I have to remind myself he's about to get me deported.

"I don't know."

"Yeah, you don't. What's your principal's name over there?"

"Sister Mary Augustus."

"She's not going to be too happy to hear about this."

"No."

"I went to Catholic school. Those nuns are no joke."

He reads the school's phone number off my student ID and dials. When someone picks up, he says he is Lieutenant Joe Gallipano of the Willow Falls Police Department. He gets put through right away.

"Yeah, Sister, I've got one of your students in the precinct here. Seems she was hanging out instead of being in class." He gives her my name.

"Yes, that's her. Oh, is that right?" He puts his hand over the mouthpiece of the phone. "So your mom works at the school, huh?"

"Yes."

"Mmmm-hmmm. Yes, sister. Sure, no problem. Right away." He hangs up. "Boy, I think you're in for it," he says. *No kidding.* "Let's go."

"Where are we going?"

"Your school. Seems like Sister Mary wants a word with you."

Wait, what?

He walks me out to the parking lot and puts me in the back of a black-on-black police car. It is scary looking as hell. There are no handles in the doors and I am in what appears to be a giant cage with a seat in it. He walks around to the driver's side and starts it up.

"You know, you're too young to be doing something so stupid," he calls back to me. "I know you think you're almost done and you're sick of it. But you don't know how many crazies are out there just waiting to find a vulnerable girl like you."

"Around here?" It is bold, but I am getting wings from the idea that maybe, just maybe, he is really just going to bust me at school and not report me to immigration. He didn't even check my name in a system or anything.

"Yes, around here. You kids walk around thinking you're just safe everywhere you go. But there are a lot of wolves out there. And you're just a helpless little sheep sitting out there in the bushes like that. That's why we're around, you know? We're like the sheepdogs."

Sheep? Sheepdogs? Huh?

He's quiet until we get to the school. He walks me inside. In the principal's office, Sister Mary Augustus and my mother are looking at me like I've just murdered the pope. But all I can think is that I am almost in the clear. Is this cop really going to leave? Leave me here and not send me to jail or Argentina or jail *then* Argentina?

"Sister, she's all yours now."

"Thank you, Officer."

"No problem at all, Sister. I'm the proud graduate of a Catholic school myself."

She seems to soften. "Then God bless you."

He takes his hat off. "And you as well."

And then he's gone.

I fight the urge to dance.

But I still have the livid-looking nun and my mother to deal with.

"Explain yourself," says Sister Mary Augustus after he's gone.

"I can't," I say.

"I should say you can't. This is unacceptable. Your grades are really suffering."

"Yes."

"I am informed that your grade point average has dropped below acceptable standards for NHS membership."

"Yes."

"And of course, we also expect our NHS members to uphold the highest values of our school. You've failed to do that."

"I have. I'm sorry."

"Consider yourself removed from the NHS effective immediately."

I am surprised by how much this hurts.

"And I'll expect you to stay for detention every day next week."

"Yes, Sister."

She turns to my mother. "Is there anything you'd like to say to her?"

She says in Spanish. "I'm only here doing this job so you can graduate. But I can't help you if you won't help yourself." I expect her to sound furious, but she just sounds like she hasn't slept in a week. So tired.

I stare at the tiles.

Finally Sister Mary Augustus says, "You can leave now. Go straight to class. I'll be watching you."

CHELSEA SITS ON HER BED PLAYING A GAME ON HER COMPUTER. Outside, her mother is taking pictures of the iris, which have bloomed. The whole length of the lawn is lit up with flowers of every color. From up here, Chelsea's mom looks ridiculously happy about it.

"So how long does this detention thing last?" says Chelsea.

"All next week."

"That's almost as bad as when you ignored me every day for Nate."

The sound of his name hurts. I leave the window and sit down on the floor, my feet up on a poofy ottoman.

"Not nice," I say.

"Well, it's true."

She looks awkward a little, like there is more to say. I think she's going to get into it with me about being the kind of girl who drops her friends for a guy.

But what she says is, "Hey, so I got my letter from Boston. I'm in."

I want to be happy for her. I don't know how to be.

"That's cool, Chels. Is that where you're going?"

"Yeah."

I let this sink over me, Chelsea gone, three states away. Everyone gone. Nate already gone. Just me and my father in that dank, dark apartment, with nothing but empty space where my grown-up life should be.

"M, what about you? What are you doing?"

"I really don't know."

"I don't understand. Can you help me understand what's up with you?"

"I don't even know," I say.

"I mean, but you have to know. You can't just be the person who gets the great grades and then just stops wanting to go to school and not knowing why, right? Is there something going on? I mean, besides the Nate thing."

"It's not Nate."

"Good, because if you're just all falling apart over a guy, I'm going to have to stage a serious intervention."

"He's not just a guy."

"No, I get it, but still. M, we've been friends since, like, the womb. You've totally got to tell me what's going on."

"I don't know how to explain it."

"Try."

I close my eyes. *Try.* I want to try. The heavy feeling of dread spreads in my chest again. *Well, see, Chelsea, I'm an illegal immigrant and I can't go to college or get a job because I have no Social Security number. And I can't think of a way out, even though I think and think about it all day. And I am too disgusted and ashamed to ask anyone what to do.*

I try to start, minus the illegal thing.

"Have you ever just wanted something to be over? But you couldn't think of a way out?"

"I'm not sure I know what you mean."

"Have you ever felt so bad, but there was no solution?"

"But *why* is there no solution, M? There is always a solution."

She's not getting it. "There is not always a solution, can you just take my word for it?"

"No. Can you explain? Is it your family? Is someone sick or something?"

"Sometimes it's complicated and it's not so easy to explain."

She gets down off her bed, sits next to me on the floor. "I don't understand."

I think maybe if I change the subject. "Why did Grady do it, do you know?"

"Grady?"

"Grady Ford. Quinn's brother."

"Oh my God, M. Is that why you're . . ." There is a total look of horror on her face.

"I'm just talking, Chels. Relax. But Grady . . . was there a solution for Grady?"

"Grady was on drugs, M. Are you on drugs?"

I laugh. "No. Don't you think you would know?"

She's still not laughing. "I'm not sure now."

"I'm just saying . . . sometimes you feel out of options."

"Do you . . . feel out of options?"

"I'm just using him as an example."

"M, you're scaring me."

I sit up to look at her.

"Try to see it from my side. Nate is gone. School sucks. You're leaving. I'm just stuck here. What are my options?"

"M, please, you're really scaring me. Please promise me you're okay."

"I'm fine."

She tilts her head sideways, looking unconvinced. "Can you just sign up for the community college? For me? Or ... do you want a job? I'll help you find a job. And maybe next year after you figure some stuff out ..."

"What if nothing is going to change next year either, Chelsea? What if this is all there is? What if there are lives like yours that go on into adulthood and others that ... don't?"

She starts to cry, just tears spilling out of her eyes. "M, please stop. Stop." She hugs me. It feels weird. "You *know* how many people love you, right?" she says. It embarrasses me. It is weirdly intimate. And I know it is untrue.

"You've been such a good friend, Chelsea. I know you're going to do great in Boston." It's all I can think to say in response.

She sobs into my shoulder. "M. Promise me you're going to be okay."

"I promise." I don't particularly mean it and she doesn't seem to believe it. But at least it ends this horrible conversation.

CHAPTER TWENTY-FIVE

In the weeks since Nate and I broke up, I have powered up my phone about 127 times a day hoping to see his number. I have been sure I would never hear his voice again.

But on Saturday morning, after I'm home, it happens.

"Hi, M, how are you?" Like nothing. It makes me want to laugh and cry.

"I'm good."

"Hey, so I wanted to know what color your prom dress is."

"My dress? Why?"

"Because there's this thing about cummerbunds matching."

"Blue," I lie. I don't have a dress. I've been pretty sure that prom thing was a way to get me out of his car, so I've been planning on skipping it.

"And are we getting a limo?" he asks.

I haven't signed up for anything yet.

"Yeah, with some friends of mine."

"Okay, so are we still on?"

"You don't have to."

"Do you have . . . do you . . . are you going with someone else?"

"No."

"So it's a date then."

I go in to the kitchen where my mother is cooking.

"Ma, I need a prom dress."

"Oh, I'm so happy you decided to go." One good thing I've got to hand to her, she has totally gotten over the school-cutting thing. And has not told my father. I'm not surprised about the school thing, but I'm shocked about the not-telling.

"Can you make me one?" I ask.

"Sure, yes. Do you want to go to the city this afternoon and buy the fabric?"

"Yes." I am grateful that she's up for quick action.

We sit on the bus as it barrels toward New York. There must be fabric stores closer, but you need a car to get anywhere in New Jersey. In New York, the fabric district is a block away from the bus terminal. My mother has a goofy grin on her face as she sits with her ankles crossed and absently plays with Jose's hair. Jose carries on a conversation with imaginary little people under the seat.

"Do you know what you want it to look like?" asks my mom.

"No, not really."

She pulls a magazine out of her frayed tote bag. It is last year's copy of a gossip magazine Oscar rundown.

"Show me on here which one you like best."

I thumb through it. They're all so gorgeous. Well, some are ridiculous, but most are amazing. I don't know what any of the other girls at school will be wearing. They've been chattering, but I haven't been paying attention. I pick a one-shouldered gown worn by an actress known more for her piercing blue eyes and knockout boobs than her Oscar-worthiness. She looks like someone I'd like to be one day.

I hand the magazine to my mother and point to it. "That one," I say. "In blue."

"I know just where to get that rhinestone buckle, too," she says. The bus hits a bump, she smiles even goofier, and Jose tells all his imaginary little bus people to hold on tight.

∞

WE HAVE BEEN HOME FOR ABOUT AN HOUR WHEN THERE ARE heavy knocks on the door. No one ever knocks on our apartment door. My mother goes to it, stands inside of it. The knock gets heavier. She looks through the peephole.

"Willow Falls Police! I'm going to need you to open the door."

She turns to look at me, her eyes wide. "Oh my God, Monse," she says, almost a whisper. The police at the apartment cannot be good news. I feel trapped.

I look at the window for a stupid minute, as if it were possible to get out that way.

Slowly, my mother opens it. She looks smaller than usual. Her hand is shaking.

The cop steps inside. I've seen him directing traffic in town. He says, "Is Monserrat your daughter?"

"Monserrat!" she calls me.

I walk over. These cops finally probably ran my name and now they're here for me.

"I'm Monse. My mom doesn't speak English."

"Spanish?"

"Yeah."

"We'll get a Spanish-speaking officer over here. In the meantime, I need to talk to you," he says to me. "Can you explain to her?"

I do.

He comes with me into the kitchen. My mom stays by the door, like she's guarding it.

The cop sits at the kitchen table and points to another chair. I sit down.

"Monserrat, is that what I call you?"

"I guess. Most people call me M.T."

"Okay, M.T., let me explain to you why we're here."

"Okay."

"We received a report that you are thinking of harming your-self. Are you thinking of harming yourself?"

My mind starts racing. The conversation with Chelsea? How would they know? Unless she told them? Did Chelsea call the cops on me? Is this whole thing going to be over because I tried to open up to my best friend? That can't be true.

"M.T., can you answer me please?"

"No."

"Let me explain something to you. People don't usually go around calling us to report something like that unless they are pretty sure there is cause for concern. So do you want to tell me what happened?"

"Nothing happened."

"Look, this is the situation. If I determine that you're a poten-tial harm to yourself, I need to take you in for assessment. Do you understand?"

"I'm not a potential harm to myself."

"So the person that called us just made that up?"

"I guess."

I hear another cop talking to my mom by the front door.

"Do you want to tell me what happened?"

"No."

"Would you rather speak to a female officer?"

"I would rather not speak to anyone. I'm fine. This is kind of ridiculous," I say, my voice a little louder than I mean for it to get.

"Just calm down, okay?"

"I'm calm. I'm just . . . I don't know what to say to you."

Another cop comes into the kitchen.

"So what do we have?"

"This young lady denies making any threats of self-harm."

"People don't just call us, you know," says the other cop. "You just broke up with your boyfriend? Not doing so well at school?"

Why would these cops know anything about that? I can't believe Chelsea.

"I do fine at school. I'm National Honor Society vice president."

"That's not what we heard."

"From who?"

"That's confidential."

"So people can just make up stories about other people and call you guys?"

The first cop leaves the room, goes over to my mother. The second cop sits down. "We're just trying to help you."

"Thanks. This is not exactly the kind of help I need."

"What kind of help *do* you need?"

"That's not what I meant."

We sit there, quietly, for five minutes that feel like hours.

Finally, the first cop comes back into the kitchen.

"So, as I was just explaining to your mother, I'm going to have you talk to some people. We're going to take you in to talk to them, and then we'll see where we're at."

My mother, standing behind him, is sobbing.

"What does that mean? You're *arresting* me? For what?"

"We're just taking you in for an evaluation."

"An evaluation of what?"

"Your mental condition."

"You can't just do that."

"The law says that when someone potentially might harm themselves, we can take them in for an evaluation. So that's what's going to happen here."

I feel the panic rising. It makes me want to run. I look at the door to the kitchen, wonder if I can bolt that way.

But maybe if I just sound reasonable. "Listen, I am not going to harm myself. I am fine. I don't know who is telling you lies. I think someone is trying to get back at me. See? I'm calm. I'm fine." But the calmer I try to look, the less calm I feel.

My mother is trying to talk to them in English. "Please. My daughter good. Everything fine. Okay? *Okay?*" The other cop is talking to her quietly in really bad, broken Spanish. Jose is hiding behind her, crying with his face buried in her hip.

"Listen, it's going to be okay," says the cop. "I'm going to need you to come with us now, and we'll have someone talk to you. Then they'll call your mom and talk to her about next steps."

I stand there, too shocked to say anything or even to move. He puts his arm on my elbow. I start walking to the door. I try to look at everything, wondering if it's the last time before they deport me. Because, of course, this is it. They're putting my name into some system and it's going to spit out that I don't belong here. And I'll be on a plane out of the country before I know it.

They put me in the back of a cop car. I figure we're going to the police station, but they keep going, past the street it's on to the highway. After about twenty minutes, he pulls up to a medical center. He parks and we walk to a door labeled "Primary Screening Center."

Inside it looks like a doctor's office. Someone comes out to get me and I sit inside a room like an examining room. I wonder if they're going to want to give me a physical or something.

Eventually, after what feels like an hour, a woman comes into the room. She's got short blond hair, a patch of it shaved by her left ear. She's got cargo pants and biker boots and a grown-up-looking pink blouse. She looks like she hasn't decided if she wants to hang on to adolescence or go on with adulthood.

"So, hey. I heard you like to be called M.T. Can I call you that?"

"Sure."

"So you know why you're here."

"Not really, no."

"You know we got a call that you'd made some statements about harming yourself. And when the police officers responded, they felt maybe you needed to be assessed. Do you understand?"

"I guess."

"Look, I know this is scary, but the best way for this to be over is for you to just talk to me straight, okay? Our job here is to decide whether you're in trouble or not."

In that case . . .

"I'm fine."

"Funny thing, that statement. It turns out that most people who are *not* fine say they *are* fine. So we're going to need to talk a little bit more than that, okay?"

"I guess. My mother must be freaking out."

"We all just want to make sure you get any help you need. If you need any. So, anyway, what about your mom? Do you want to tell me anything about her?"

"No."

"Okay. So what do you want to talk about?"

"I want to talk about going home."

"You like it at home?"

"I guess. It's fine. I'm seventeen. Do you talk to a lot of seventeen-year-olds who like it at home?"

"I talk to a lot of everybody. But let's focus on you. How are things at home?"

"Fine."

"I'm getting a lot of 'fine's out of you."

"Because that's how it is."

"So you want to tell me why you told your best friend that you wanted to kill yourself?"

There it is. Chelsea. I can't believe it.

"That's not what happened."

"She just made that up?"

"She misunderstood."

"Tell me how someone misunderstands, 'I want to kill myself.'"

"I never said that. Not those words."

"What *did* you say?"

"Nothing. We were just talking about next year and I was kind of trying to explain how everything is going to be different. She's going to college."

"But not you?"

"No."

"Why?"

"Jesus, is that grounds for being held here?"

"I'm just trying to understand what's going on."

"Nothing is going on."

"You keep saying that."

"I don't know how to convince you otherwise."

"Maybe that's the problem. Maybe if you stop trying to convince me and just start telling me what's up, we'll get somewhere."

I just stare at the little patch of shaved hair by her left ear.

She stands up. "Okay, listen, there is a bunch of paperwork associated with this kind of hold. So I'm going to send in a nurse to ask you some questions. Child Protective Services will probably be here in a few hours. And I need to have you assessed by a psychiatrist, too. So it's likely that you're going to be here overnight."

"*What?* Overnight?"

"Yeah, I'm sorry, I know it's a bummer. But we can't get through all the assessments we need to get through right now. It's Saturday night."

"But then I can go home tomorrow?"

"Maybe. I don't know. Let's worry about that tomorrow."

"What do you mean *you don't know*?"

"It depends on the assessments, the determinations we make about whether you're a threat to yourself."

"And if you decide I am?"

"We can hold you, yeah."

"How long?"

"Let's not worry about that, okay? Just talk to the nurse and let's do this one step at a time."

She takes me down the hall to another room. This one has a bed in it. It's got no sheets. A silver toilet sits in the corner.

"This is a cell," I say to her.

"It's just a place where you can rest for a while if you want."

"I don't want to be here."

"I know how this can feel. Let's just have you talk to the people you need to talk to. You'll be fine, okay?"

I sit on the bed. I can't believe I'm in this terrifying place.

CHAPTER TWENTY-SIX

talk to nurses. I talk to Child Protective Services. I talk to a guy with an impossibly large mole on his face. I tell them what I think they want to hear. Finally, the lights go out in the room. I put my head down. I'm cold, but they won't give me a blanket. I tuck my arms up into my shirt. I close my eyes. Sleeping is impossible. I wonder about my mother, what a mess she must be. I imagine Jose thinking I am some sort of criminal, that I did something wrong and that's why the cops took me away. And maybe they've all been put into their cells already now that I was stupid enough to bring us to the attention of the police. Maybe they're all sleeping on a cot in a detention center somewhere too. I am such a loser. It is all my fault.

I imagine Nate seeing me here. It feels like years ago that I was shopping for the fabric for my prom dress. Now I won't make it to prom. I won't make it to graduation. I won't make it anywhere I want to go. I thought I had seen the worst of how things could be, but now I managed to make them even more of a mess.

In the morning, they bring me breakfast. Even if it didn't look so gross, I couldn't eat it. I drink the little container of orange juice.

Finally Patch comes back.

"Hey," she says. Like we're about to go to the mall together or something.

"Hey," I say.

"I wanted to see how you were doing this morning."

"I want to go home is how I'm doing."

She laughs. "I get it. But let's just go through things again, okay?"

"Okay."

"I know it's a pain, but I just can't help but feel like there is something you're not telling me."

"There isn't."

"There is. You weren't saying good-bye to your friend because she's going to college four months from now."

"I was."

"I don't think that was it. Do you see why that sounds like you're going to kill yourself? A lot of people who are about to commit suicide say their good-byes."

"That's not what I was doing."

"The way I see it, you've got a lot of the signs. Fatigue and loss of energy. You told Dr. Warren about that. Withdrawal from family and friends. Loss of interest in activities. The way your grades are plummeting. So I want you to tell me what's up."

She's relentless. She won't stop. Maybe if I tell her a little something, she will go way already. Or better yet, let me go away.

"I am sad, I'm frustrated, but I'm not going to kill myself."

"You don't think about it?"

"No. I mean, I don't want to say yes and then you lock me up in here forever. I don't think about it like I actually want to do it. I just want a solution."

"To what?"

"To a lot of things."

"Like what? Give me one."

"I can't."

"Why?"

"Because bad things could happen to me and to my family."

"Like what bad things?"

"Like, if I tell you about us . . . are you going to arrest me?"

"Arrest you for what? Have you committed a crime?"

"I think so, yeah."

"If you want a lawyer, we can make sure you talk to one."

"I don't think a lawyer could help me."

"Why?"

I might as well. She knows already anyway. I just want to get it over with.

"I'm illegal."

"Illegal? You mean undocumented?"

"Yeah."

"I don't care about your immigration status. That's not a crime anyway. Is that what you meant when you said 'crime'?"

"Yeah. But, wait, you seriously don't care about my immigration status?"

"No."

I can't believe it. I put my face in my hands and the sobs come hard. Sudden. I feel the fear washing out of me, leaving me more tired than I've felt in a long time, but a little exhilarated, too. After a few more sobs, I'm not sure I'm going to be able to suck air through my nose again. I've never said this out loud before, and certainly not to someone who probably has the number to the people who could have me kicked out of the country programmed into her cell phone. I've imagined—dreaded—this moment a thousand times, but I've never thought it would be like this, with her saying that my immigration status doesn't matter to her.

She puts her hand on the back of my shoulder. That makes me cry some more.

"Is that why you don't want to talk to us?"

"You're going to tell the cops about me and they're going to deport me and my whole family."

"We're here to help. We don't do that. You want some water?"

"Yes."

She gets me some. It feels good, so cool going down.

"So now you want to tell me what's up?"

"That's what I meant when I was talking to Chelsea. That her life could go forward but not mine."

"Because you're undocumented. But you didn't tell her that."

"I can't tell her that. I can't tell anyone."

"But you told me."

"Because I figured I was done anyway. Might as well."

She laughs. "You're never done. So no one knows?"

"No."

"That must be a pretty heavy thing to carry around."

"I guess, yeah."

"So do you want to die?" she asks.

"No. Look, to be honest, yes, I've thought about it, just kind of running all the options through my head. But not because I have a plan or because I want to die. I just want it stop being so hard. Do you understand what I mean?"

"Yeah."

"Can I go home, then?"

"Yeah. I'm going to let you go today. But let's talk a little longer first, maybe about some options. A little bit of a plan for you, okay?"

"Okay."

MY FATHER PICKS ME UP IN THE BORROWED CAR. IT IS A CHEERY, sunny afternoon, which makes his mood all the darker. I reach for the backseat passenger's side door, but he pushes open the front-seat door. "Up front," he says. I get in.

He starts driving, his jaw twitching. He's on the highway before he says anything. I wonder how far away he feels he needs to drive before he lets me have it good. I brace for a smack. I am on high alert, willing my face-covering reflexes to be faster than his hand.

"You think this is funny?"

"No."

"You know we could have all gotten deported because of this?"

"I didn't mean for anything to happen."

"You didn't mean. You didn't *mean*. That's your excuse for all your selfishness."

"I just was talking to a friend of mine. She misunderstood me. It got out of hand."

"Oh, okay. So now you're telling people about our private business."

"No. I was just telling her that I was sad that she's going away to college and I won't see her."

"I suppose you're telling these people lies about me, that I don't treat you right?"

"You *don't* treat me right."

"Is that what you've been telling them?"

"I didn't say anything about you."

"Because you know if you get me deported, that means your mother and your brother go, too. Even if they let you stay."

"I didn't say anything."

"You better watch your step. Keep your mouth shut. These people in this country are not your friends."

"Are *you* my friend?"

"You don't know anything. You want to stay here so much. For what?"

"Don't you understand that I've never been anywhere else? Is it so weird for you to get that this is where I grew up? I wouldn't know anything, not enough Spanish to make it in school, not the money, not the system, not how to get a job. Nothing."

"All I know is that you never learn. Let me tell you something. Things are not going to end well between you and me."

CHAPTER TWENTY-SEVEN

Prom night comes and I haven't eaten in two days. I am in a full-on panic. Everything is riding on this night. If I act happy, then maybe Nate and I have another shot. Maybe I can hold on to one thing that doesn't stink.

I try to do my hair like the actress in the picture. I achieve seventy-eight percent success. Mine doesn't look as shiny or as solid, but it makes pretty waves by my ear. I do my makeup a little heavier than usual, but not too much. At least I hope not too much.

My mother is hand-stitching the hem of the dress twenty minutes before Nate is supposed to show up.

"Ma, hurry up."

"I'm almost done, hold on."

She runs an iron over it and hands it to me. I put it on. It fits perfectly.

"I swear you've lost weight since I measured you," she says.

I turn around and look at my butt, then back to my front. It's kind of crazy how my mom has made an exact replica of the dress in the magazine just by looking at it. She's gotten the right fabric, the right rhinestone buckle, everything.

She's doing that mothery, teary thing. *She's about to say I'm so beautiful.*

"You're so beautiful. You're a woman," she says. On cue.

I give her a weird little half hug to hold off her tears. It doesn't work.

"Ma, zipper me up; he's going to be here any minute."

She holds my face in her hands. They're rough. "You have a great time tonight, okay?"

I need to pry her off me before she goes in for another hug. "Okay, okay, hurry."

She presses some bills into my hands. I'm wondering where she's scoring the cash suddenly. I'm carrying a little evening bag that she pulled out of some forgotten corner of her closet. It's a little retro, but in a cool way. The shoes I borrowed pinch at the back of my foot.

I run down the stairs without checking if Nate is outside. But he is. He looks amazing in his tux. Although we didn't compare blues, his cummerbund matches my sapphire-colored dress perfectly.

"Hey," he says. Like he just saw me yesterday.

"Hey," I say back. I think of the Post-it notes. In my Nate box in my room.

"Thank God it wasn't light blue. I wondered after I got this. Somehow I knew you'd wear dark blue. You look amazing," he says, smiling.

"Where are your glasses?" I ask.

"Contacts. I hate them, but I thought for tonight they'd be better."

He looks different—older, a little bit—with no glasses and a shorter haircut.

He opens his door for me.

We drive to Dakota's, where we're all meeting.

Dakota's house is done all in Zen minimalist style—white carpets, modern white couches. There is one lone giant red circle in a painting on the far wall of a huge great room, over a fireplace surrounded by white stone. No wonder she's like a Swiss watch, this girl. I bet she hasn't even been allowed to spill anything since she was three years old. I've known her all my school life and I've never been in her house before. It's not a very kid-friendly place.

Her mom is severely skinny. It doesn't help that her platinum blond hair is cut in a straight line and flat-ironed to within an inch of its slick little life and sprayed to death on her head. She takes pictures of each couple by the fireplace, then all of us outside by her Japanese garden. Then it's time to go.

In the limo, Dakota pulls out a flask from her bag. A couple of the others do, too.

"Okay, people, it's time to fuel up," says Dakota. Wow. Talk about never really knowing someone.

I glance over at Nate. I wonder what it's going to take to get him to love me again. I feel like this is my only chance. A little liquid courage. I take a long, burning swig.

The prom itself is pure cheese, at a local catering hall done with too many shiny columns. There is fast dancing for hours. And slow dancing for a little while. During one of the slow dances I nestle my face in Nate's neck and try to inhale him without being too creepy. God, I love the smell of him. It's amazing how a person can smell different from absolutely everyone else on the planet.

After the slow song, I leave him at the table to go to the bathroom. It's almost time to go to our after-party.

One of the girls is handing out some pills. Quinn Ford, who should have known better than to wear a green dress but didn't, takes one. I'm not sure what they are, but the drinks from the car are wearing off, so I take one, too. I sit in the bathroom for a while, trying to strategize how best to get Nate back.

Chelsea walks in. I have been avoiding her all night. In fact, I haven't talked to her since that sleepover at her house and her total betrayal. She's tried calling me and cornering me at school.

She says, "M, please, I *have* to talk to you."

"I think I've told you enough times that I don't want to talk to you."

"M, I'm sorry. Can you please just let me explain?"

I'm wondering if that tingling in my left arm is from the pill or something else. I get up. I wobble a little. I get in her face, close.

"I never want to speak to you again, okay? Get it?"

Her eyes get wide and she steps back half a step. I know I don't mean that. But I can't have her pestering me, not tonight, not while I am trying to make Nate see how much fun I can be. How I'm not gloomy at all. I can't do that if Chelsea makes me cry remembering just how she betrayed me, how bad she could have made things for me.

I walk out of the bathroom and back to my Nate.

After prom is over, Dakota tells the driver to head into the city. She seems to have managed to smuggle half a liquor store into the limo, because she keeps the drinks coming. By now I am a warrior goddess, and my powers come from the liquid that has long since stopped burning. I am Good. I am Exciting. I am Fun. I am Not Gloomy. Not the downer Nate ran away from.

Nate loves me again. I just know it.

We get inside the little dive. The music is tinny but earsplitting. I drag Nate onto the dance floor. I trip on something. Floorboard or something.

"M, are you okay?"

"I'm great, Nate. Ha! Get it? Great? Nate? Let's dance."

"You don't seem to be doing so well."

"I'm doing amazing."

"Can we sit and talk for a little while?"

"Oh, talking is for losers, come *on*, let's dance." I need to move, move, move. I can't stand the thought of talking.

"Since when do you drink this way, M?" asks Nate.

"Don't be an old man. You wanted fun, right? You wanted happy. Look at me. I'm happy! Let's go." I tug him.

He gets on the dance floor and dances. I look at his eyes. He looks at a point somewhere past my left ear. He pulls me in a little closer.

On the ride home, Dakota is still going like a champ. I want to keep up, but there is a shrill, strange note in my ear that won't go away. Everyone else stays at Dakota's house, but I ask Nate if we can go for a ride.

"Sure, where to?" he asks when we're in his car.

"Summer Park."

He drives there, pulls into the parking lot. In the same spot where we exchanged Christmas presents.

Nate puts his hand on mine. "Did you have fun?"

"Well, there's one thing missing," I say. I channel my inner seductress. I imagine what the actress who wore this dress to the Oscars would say in a situation like this. I lean over and kiss him. The car spins a little.

He kisses back, and it's just like I remember it. We kiss some more, his hands moving down my neck, to my shoulders, to my back. I want him to go further. I've decided that tonight is the night. I touch him there, hoping that will spur him on. It doesn't. He kisses, but doesn't advance.

"Nate, I love you. Even if we're not together, I want you to be my first. Let's do it tonight." Maybe, after this, he will want to stay.

He pulls back, takes off my rhinestone barrette, puts it back in tighter. He kisses my temple. "I can't, M."

"Why?"

"Because we're not together and I wouldn't feel right."

"But I'm telling you it can be like this, no strings, just so that I can remember that you were my first."

"I'm sorry, I can't. Not like this." I think that's pity in his eyes.

I sit back in his seat. Suddenly the car spins violently. I feel really sick to my stomach.

I just make it out of the car before I throw up all over the hem of my Oscar knockoff dress and my borrowed shoes.

CHAPTER TWENTY-EIGHT

The sun feels vicious, like it's trying to stab me. I let my bike roll with as little effort as possible. Thank goodness for all the flat land on the way to the library. I'm only out in this horrid sunshine because it hurts more to stay in my tomb of an apartment than it does to fight my hangover.

I lock my bike to the rack. Go inside. I get online. No email. I get on Facebook and check my feed.

The latest story is Quinn, something about a vigil tonight. Who in the world has energy for a vigil the night after prom? Talk about religious fanatics.

I scroll down. Patricia's going to this stupid vigil, too. Thirty-two people have commented on her status.

I scroll down past all the vigil nonsense to see posts from last night. A bunch of phone pictures uploaded. Our table. Me sitting on Nate's lap. Me in the limo. Man, did my eyeliner really run like that? I quickly save them to my hard drive, to a folder named Him.

I scroll back up to this vigil thing and read through the comments on Patricia's post.

Patricia: We'll be meeting at 7:00 p.m. in front of the school. Bring your own candles.

Jane: I can't believe it.

Siobhan: I will miss this but will be down tomorrow after my finals. I'll be saying a prayer, too.

How in the world is Siobhan friends with Patricia and crew?

Kelly: It's just so crazy. Please pray for Chelsea.

Jane O'Hara: Thanks, everyone, for the good wishes for Chelsea. She is strong. I will keep you all posted on here as much as I can.

Pray for Chelsea for what?

As I'm trying to get the story, a message pops up. It's Josh.

"I just heard," he says.

"Just heard what?" I ask.

"About Chelsea."

"What about Chelsea?"

"You didn't hear?"

"No."

"Car accident last night. This morning, actually."

"After prom, you mean?"

"Yeah. Hit by a drunk driver."

"She's okay?"

"I don't think so."

"Where is she?"

"I'm not sure the name of the hospital."

"Can you ask Siobhan?"

"I'll ask."

I call Dakota. No answer. I call Patricia. Nothing. I have to call five people before finally I get Kathy from history on the phone.

"I just heard about Chelsea. Where is she?"

"Mid-Bergen General," she says. "But you can't go see her."

"Why?"

"Not even family is getting in. She's in intensive care. Last we heard she had just gotten out of some kind of surgery. Friend her mom. She's posting updates on her page."

CHAPTER TWENTY-NINE

The entrance to the hospital is lit up with fancy lamps and covered in dark wood. There is a gift shop filled with teddy bears and stuff, just the right balance of cute and serious. This place looks like what I imagine a hotel would look like, if I'd ever been in one. What they look like on TV.

The walk to Chelsea's room takes forever, through corridors that say we're in a different wing, then another. Then an elevator. Then more walking. Finally, Chelsea's mom and I are there.

Chelsea looks like the cartoon version of the accident victim—casts, the pulley over the bed. Her eyes are closed, the left side of her face covered with a yellowing bruise. I thought her mom said she was going to be okay? She looks like she's in a coma.

Her mom pats her hand. "Hey, Chels, I'm here."

Is she going to do that whole depressing, "I know you're in a coma but I know you can hear me" thing? Because I don't think I can take that.

But Chelsea opens her eyes. "Hey, Ma." She looks just like she does when she wakes up from a sleepover. Well, except for the hospital gear. And the bruises. She looks over at me. "M, you came."

"Chels, what happened?"

"You know how I drive." She laughs.

"Does it hurt?"

"They've got me on the good stuff."

Her mom says, "I'm going to go say hello to the nurses."

I inch closer to Chelsea. She looks in my eyes. "You're not mad at me anymore?" she says.

"No."

"See the lengths to which I'll go to make you forgive me."

I smile at her cheesy joke.

The next time I visit Chelsea I find a two-bus combination that goes to Mid-Bergen. I take it there every day. I sit on her bed and talk about nothing. The reality star who had the baby with the soccer player and named him after a tropical fruit. The strange bugs eating the bushes outside of school. I paint her nails and reach for her lip gloss for her. That's all I can handle for now.

One day when I get there, I am surprised to see Siobhan sitting next to the bed.

"Oh, hey, you're busy," I say, backing up.

"No, come in. It's just Siobhan," says Chelsea.

Yeah, I know.

"Oh, hi," I say.

Siobhan nods in my direction.

"How are you?" I ask to no one in particular, hoping Chelsea will answer.

"Oh, well, I'm running a marathon later," jokes Chelsea.

"Awesome."

"Siobhan here, a little worse."

"Oh? I'm sorry." I seriously don't want to hear about Siobhan's issues.

"She broke up with Josh," says Chelsea.

Siobhan glares at her, like she wasn't supposed to tell, but Chelsea doesn't seem to notice.

"Oh," I say. Just because I have no idea what else to say.

We talk for a while but I feel really awkward with Siobhan just sitting there. She barely says two words. How long is long enough to not seem rude? I wait an hour, then tell Chelsea I need to go. I say good-bye to them both, and head to the elevator. I'm surprised when Siobhan calls out to wait for her.

She's red.

"M, so I wanted to talk to you."

"Okay."

"Why did you pretend in there that you didn't already know about Josh and me?"

"Ummm . . . because I didn't." I say this slowly, like explaining something to a child who's not getting it.

"Right. I know about you two."

"You know *what* about us two?"

"I know you've been talking all year."

"We've been Facebook friends since Chelsea and I went up and met him that weekend. I think Chelsea's friends with him, too."

"Oh, don't try to play it off like that. You think you're so much better than me. Just because you're all jock and bike everywhere to get nice legs. Just because I put on the freshman ten and you probably think that's funny. You're so above everyone."

This is awkward. Where did this come from?

"Siobhan, honestly, I don't know what you're talking about, and I don't know why you're getting in my face like this."

"So you're going to deny he's coming down to New Jersey this summer to be with you?"

"Are you kidding?"

"I read his Facebook messages. I know that you guys have been talking. I know he told you he's coming down."

"You hacked his Facebook account? Not cute."

"That's not really an answer."

"I don't have to give you any answers. I'm not even sure what the question is."

"Is he coming down because of you?"

"No. If you think I'm trying to get your boyfriend, you're crazy."

"Why, because he's not good enough for you? Maybe he doesn't seem like much to you, but I really love him. Loved him. And anyway, what kind of a pretentious name is M.T. anyway? You're just too cool for everyone. And you've been a total jerk to Chelsea."

Then she starts bawling. It's pretty horrifying to see. I stare at her shoes. Gold moccasins. They shock me a little. They seem out of character. She wipes her face with the outside edges of her hands, the left one for the right side, the right one for the left. I focus on those moccasins. I almost feel like saying something nice.

"Don't cry," is the best I can think of.

"Yeah, real easy for you to say."

CHAPTER THIRTY

Chelsea comes home in June. She's on crutches, and her leg is still in a cast. They put pins in her. From now on, every time she goes to an airport, she's going to have to carry a letter from her doctor explaining why she sets off the metal detectors. I think that's kind of awesome.

We are sitting in Chelsea's room. She props her cast up on a pillow that looks like a mini sack of grain.

She says, "M, can we talk about the thing about you said? About . . . not having a future? And what I did? I really didn't mean to hurt you."

Maybe Chelsea found the strength that comes from being home. Or maybe it's just time.

I take a deep breath. "Okay. But, first, can I tell you something?

"Yes."

"You know I can't go to college."

"You can explain the problem with the grades at the end. I mean, you've got three and a half years of great grades."

"No, it's not that. I'm going to tell you something."

THE SECRET SIDE OF EMPTY

"Okay."

"So . . . my parents came over when I was little, and they didn't have permission to stay. So we're illegals."

"Like . . . you don't have papers to be here?"

"Yeah." Chelsea's quiet for a long while.

"Why didn't you ever tell me?"

"I was so embarrassed. And my parents always said not to tell anyone, because they can use it against you."

"You know I would never do that. That's so weird that I never knew that about you."

"I know."

"I don't understand why you never told me. It's no big deal."

"It's kind of a big deal to me. That's why I was so mad when you told the cops what I said and all that crazy stuff happened."

"What happened anyway?"

"I kind of don't want to talk about it. But the cops came, and I thought I was going to get deported."

"They wouldn't do that. Why would they do that?"

"I don't know; that's what my dad always says. And I've read stories online of women calling the cops for domestic violence, then getting deported because the cops found out they were undocumented. Stuff like that."

"I'm sure that can't be true."

"I don't even know what's true anymore. I've just been so afraid to talk about it with anyone."

"I'm so sorry. I was just so scared for you. Can I ask you a question?"

"Sure."

"That day . . . were you talking about killing yourself?"

"Yes and no. It's complicated. But when the cops came they took me to a hospital for an evaluation."

"That's so scary. I'm so sorry."

"Yeah. But it helped in a weird way. It really helped me get clear about what I want. What I want is just to feel better."

"It never in a million years occurred to me that it would go so far, like hospitals and stuff. I figured they'd just have someone at school talk to you or something."

"I know."

"Now we've got to fix this illegal thing." She winks. "Marry me!" she holds out her arms, the two good limbs she's got. I slap her hand five.

"While we're confessing," says Chelsea.

"Yeah?"

"My parents are getting divorced."

"*What*? Why?"

"That day you came over and my mother talked to you. The"

day she was digging up the lawn. You remember that?"

"Yeah."

"She thought that you knew something. But you didn't know."

"No."

"I never said anything. I didn't know how to tell you. My mother filed the papers, like, a month ago. And what sucks is that my mother inherited our house so it's my dad who's got to move out."

"That's . . . I don't know what to say. What happened with them?"

"My mother was in love with someone else. *Is*, I guess. That morning, the day she was wrecking the lawn, my parents had just this horrible fight. My father crying and telling her he still loved her. And her saying that she was very sorry, but she was in love with someone else."

"I had no idea."

"Well, I guess we're even," says Chelsea, smiling a smile which, for the first time, I realize doesn't tell the whole story.

walk into Mr. A's class with my backpack empty except for the paper I've written, on time, as I promised I would.

Mr. A starts class. "Very well, ladies, today is the day your world view papers are due. As discussed, we will be presenting them orally, then discussing them as a class. We will take the week for that. Any volunteers? Who would like to go first?"

I raise my hand. I feel good, one moment in which I know just what I want to do. Mr. A seems unsurprised and kind of pleased that I've volunteered.

"M.T., won't you start us off?"

I walk up to the podium slowly, my paper in my hand. I shift my uniform skirt off to the left a little and flatten the front of my shirt. I look over the group, mostly girls I've known since we were little—Quinn with her dead brother's license, Dakota with her unexpected drinking habits—and I realize that just the same way they don't know me, I don't know them, either.

"My paper is entitled 'Seventeen Ways to Say Illegal.'"

I hear a little rustle through the group and Mr. A shifts in his seat.

"There is this song. It's called 'Seventeen Ways to Say I'm Leaving.' It's about a girl who is thinking about suicide. Which, I guess, I've kind of done."

Dakota casts a sidelong glance at Quinn.

"I realize now, I didn't really relate to it because I wanted to die. Just because I wanted it to stop. You know? My life, I mean. The way it was. Like I had no future. Not a future like you guys, anyway. Because I am an illegal immigrant."

More chatter. I am surprised just how good it feels to say it to this group of girls who have known me—but not known me—for so long.

"So, my end-of-year essay is just a list, really. I am seventeen. And I thought it would be good to have one phrase for every year I've lived as an illegal immigrant. So, anyway, my Seventeen Ways to Say Illegal are:

  Broken

  Alone

  Not allowed

  Wrong

  Trapped

  Shunned

  Unwanted

Not good enough

Apart

A secret

On the wrong side

Misplaced

A threat

A mistake

Voiceless

Unheard

And last,

Still here anyway."

Quinn's eyes get wide and Dakota does a little clap until she realizes no one else is clapping.

I close my eyes and take a deep breath. The silence feels right somehow.

CHAPTER THIRTY-TWO

My dress for graduation is cream colored and looks like something a secretary would wear. This one my mother made slowly, for months, but only gave to me a week ago. Like everything she makes, it fits perfectly. She also gets me a pair of cream-colored high heels. She believes that shoes make the outfit. I wish I'd given her enough notice so she could have scored me a pair for prom.

We line up in the area behind the stage in the small gym that doubles as an auditorium. There are only fifty-four of us graduating. Still, we're cramped. Ms. Cronell fusses with her NHS girls, straightening sashes and pins over gowns. I don't wear either. I am still surprised it feels bad to look at them. I shift my cap. My bobby pins dig into my scalp. I am sweaty under my polyester graduation gown.

Music starts and we file onto the stage the way we've practiced. We sit in chairs. Camera flashes start to go off like a rock star just stepped onstage. I look around and see my mother standing in a corner in the back, holding Jose's hand. She waves. I smile blankly but pretend I'm smiling at nothing.

There's a lot of blabber, most of which I don't listen to. Dakota gives the valedictorian's speech. I wonder what mine would have been like if I hadn't let my grades go. Hers is something about a responsibility to the future. She seems pretty lively. I wonder if she has her magic flask with her.

Finally, The Moment We've All Been Waiting For. Sister Mary Augustus calls us up, one by one, hands us a diploma, and shakes our hand. We're supposed to stop, frozen, photo op moment, her left hand on our right shoulder, as our eager parents stand at the foot of the stage and snap pictures. When she calls Chelsea's name, everyone stands and claps. Chelsea's mother walks up from the first row and accepts her diploma on Chelsea's behalf, with everyone standing up and cheering. When my turn comes, I walk up to Sister Mary Augustus. We freeze, me with an uncomfortable glare, Sister Mary Augustus with her identi-smile. We pause there, awkwardly suspended. No one takes a picture. My mother is in the back, and waves again. She doesn't know the rules. Also, she doesn't own a camera.

And I'm a high school graduate.

We stand around and talk, girls holding big armfuls of flowers. Caps off now. Everyone is going to restaurants with parents, grandparents, cousins, siblings. A few people are having get-togethers at home.

Quinn walks up to me. "Hey, Mouse, can I talk to you?"

Every once in a while, when she wants to piss me off, she calls me by the kindergarten name. Strangely, it doesn't make me mad today. It makes me almost wistful, like throwing away a tattered old toy I haven't played with in years.

"Okay."

She walks off to the side of the auditorium where it's quiet. I follow her.

"So that was quite the bombshell in class the other day," Quinn says.

"I guess."

"It kind of puts me in a confessional mood, too."

"Yeah?"

"I mean, not so much a confession, I guess. Just . . . I want you to know that I didn't call the cops to hurt you or anything."

"What do you mean?"

"When Chelsea told me what you said to her . . . I didn't call the cops to be a jerk."

"Wait, Chelsea told you? And *you* called the cops?"

"Yeah. You didn't know?"

"No."

"She was scared and . . . I guess I'm the resident expert on the subject, you know? She called me to ask what she should do. She's so mad at me now. I told her to just tell you it was me. You hate me anyway. I didn't want you to be mad at her. You *shouldn't* be mad at her. I did it."

"I don't hate you."

"Ever since that red marker."

"It was a silver crayon."

"Whatever, Mousy Rat," she says and smiles. Then she looks off and the thousand-mile stare looks so funny on her little face. "You know, my brother gave all his comic books to his best friend and his bike to his girlfriend. The day before he . . . anyway, he told them all goodbye. Not me, though. Not my brothers. Just his friends. But none of them ever said anything to anyone."

"I didn't know."

"Yeah, anyway, so that's why."

"I guess I should say thank you. But that would be weird."

"Yeah. But then you're kind of a weirdo," she says, smiles again, and walks away.

For a minute I stand alone, playing it over in my mind. Then I go find my mother. She hugs me. "Congratulations, Monse. I'm so proud of you. You did it." Then in English she says, "A high school graduate." Her accent is so strong, but she gets all the sounds right.

"Thanks."

"I'm sorry I didn't get flowers. I didn't know that was something you were supposed to do."

"No, whatever. It's fine."

"These American customs. You know."

"I know."

"So are you going to go home now?"

"I guess."

"Okay, I'm going back to work then."

"Okay."

Jose pulls on my graduation gown. "You look really pretty," he says.

I pick him up, hold him like I used to when he was a toddler. He's still just about as light.

"So what do you do after high school?" he asks. Like he's asked a thousand times before.

"I have no idea." Like I've thought a thousand times before.

Biking home in a dress is a real pain.

CHAPTER THIRTY-THREE

It feels like we're wading through soup, an angry bruise of a sky swirling above us as we walk home from the bus stop to the apartment. Jose, who rarely whines, is whining. I am holding my brand-new Argentinian passport in the back pocket of my jean shorts. My mom had insisted that we go into the city to the Argentinian consulate to get a passport of my own, separate from hers. I think it's dumb, but I went along. Even though it's not from the country I want it to be, I'm happy to have my first grown-up document. Add it to my high school diploma, and I guess I'm officially an adult.

When we walk into the apartment, the atmosphere is even thicker inside. My father is sitting in the living room in a robe, staring off into space. As we step through the door, he says, "Where the hell have you been?" His mood is as dark as I've ever seen it. He is not used to my mother going anywhere without telling him first.

"Oh, hello, Jorge. I thought you were at work," says my mom, and it's more than a little bit of an accusation.

"I said. Where. Have. You. Been?"

"We went to get Monse her own passport."

"Well, isn't that special. Your very own passport, huh? And now you're a big high school graduate, too. I guess you must think you're something," he says.

I look away. And wait for it.

"I asked you a question!"

"No."

"No? You don't think you're better than me?"

"No."

"I think yes, you do. I see it in your snotty attitude. *Look at me when I talk to you!*"

I look at him. I know there is no way out of this without a beating. I know the signs well—the twitch of his eyebrow, the menacing way he's trying to look bigger. I can almost feel his mood, hot like the stagnant air around us. It breathes like pure frustration and hatred.

I just want to avoid another beating. *Not another one.* I am done, so sick of trying so hard to get the formula that makes it stop, but never finding it. Not silence. Not defiance. Not truth. Not lies. Nothing makes the hitting stop when he decides he's going to hit.

I get up and go to my room. I put the passport on top of a stack of books. I will take it to Chelsea's house tomorrow. It will be safer there.

He screams, "Get over here."

I go back into the living room.

"Where is your passport?" he asks. His face is contorted.

"Why?" I ask.

"Why? *Why?* Because I asked, is why! You will go in your room, and you will hand that passport to me right now."

"No." I don't know where that comes from.

He looks like I just shocked him with a taser or something. Little fish mouth. For a second it's almost comical.

"What did you say?"

"No." I don't even care about the passport. I care about making a stand. Somehow I just know that today, here, is it.

He gets ice cold, logical, like he's about to explain a math concept. "This is how it's going to go. You're going to go in your room and get me your passport. You're going to hand it to me. And if you don't. I'm. Going. To. Kill. You." Then he turns calmly to my mother. "And if you try to stop me, I'm going to kill you first. With my bare hands."

Quietly, his back and his little hands touching the wall, Jose starts to cry.

My mother grabs my hand. "Monse, please, just go get your passport. It will be fine; just don't argue."

I walk into my room. I've given up more before. The passport doesn't matter. I close my eyes and say this to myself a couple of times. I walk over to the passport. I hold it in my hands and stare at it.

It doesn't matter. But even as I tell that to myself, I don't believe it. It's a strange little hill to hold, this passport. But maybe this passport is the only thing I have that says I'm me. The truth of me, that I am here.

I won't turn it over.

I open it, and start to tear sheets out of it. I remember the woman at the consulate saying not to let any pages get torn out of it, because that makes it invalid. I know he is stronger, and he will get the passport. But he won't get it in any usable form.

My mother walks into my room and stands in the doorway. I look up at her as I tear out another sheet. She strangles a sob. "Oh my God, Monse."

The sound alerts him. He comes into my room and pushes her out of the way. His eyes land on my passport, jagged pages jutting out of it.

"Are you crazy?" he screams. "*Are you crazy?*"

"You wanted the passport. You've got the passport." I hold it out to him.

He smacks it out of my hand. The pages flutter to the floor. The swing of his arm rips the model airplane clean off its plastic wire. I hear it clatter to the floor. A wing smashes off. He's got a crazier look in his eyes than usual. He grabs a fistful of my hair. He starts to hit me in the back of the head. His fist hurts worse than anything I've ever felt before, like a rock pounding into the hardness of my head with the skin of my scalp caught in between, getting pummeled. I don't think he's ever hit me closed-fist like this.

I'm not going to stand here and take it this time. I have to hit back. I swat at him, but he's got at least half a foot of reach on me. From the angle he's holding my hair, I can't even twist around to hit back. He is hitting me hard. My mother is screaming. Jose yells, "Stop! Stop!" My father shifts his weight, knocks the lamp over. I feel things in my head rattling from his punches. It hurts, bones that aren't supposed to move feeling like they're scraping out of the way, little explosions in my head. It hurts.

But suddenly, it doesn't.

It is the freakiest thing, but now I can't feel it at all. I am numb, weirdly happy, at peace. The quiet sounds like you feel when you put your ears underwater. I float up to the ceiling, looking down on the whole scene. I see my room, my futon half open, the lamp knocked over where my father kicked it down. I see the passport pages scattered on the floor. I see Jose's SpongeBob pillow on his bed. I see the stack of papers, scattered, the books all over the place. They don't matter. Nothing matters. It is so peaceful here, by the ceiling. It is heavenly quiet. I watch a man punching a girl, her body doubled over while he punches. I have love for her, but I am free of her. I am free.

And then the moment is over. My mother gives him a shove, and I'm not sure how, but she knocks him off me. I screech back into my body. All the sound comes back, and it's ugly—screams, cries, grunts. My brother is hysterical.

But there is something else, a juice that runs through me. I am alive. It feels amazing.

I run.

I go down to the first floor, to the Cheese Lady. I pound on her door. She opens. I fall inside, slam her door behind me.

"What's the matter?" she asks.

"I need your phone."

"What happened?"

"I just . . . I need to call the police."

I wait for the cops outside. They're here in a couple of minutes. Nothing much happens in Willow Falls, so it doesn't take them long. The back of my head throbs. I reach in my hair and pull out big handfuls where he held it.

The cop walks up. He is enormously tall, with an upturned nose and icy blue eyes. He has hands the size of dinner plates. He is wearing scary storm-trooper pants. He only has about a quarter inch of hair buzz cut all over his head. In the friend-or-foe contin-uum, he definitely looks closer to foe.

"What's the situation?" he asks.

I take a deep breath. "I just . . . my father was hitting me and I just needed help." He gets some details from me—my name, address, my father's name—and writes them all down. His badge and his uniform still look dangerous to me, like the enemy who could undo me. But I push that aside and try to find the real enemy in my mind. I calm down and tell him what happened.

"Did you want to press charges?" he asks.

"No, I just want you to go upstairs with me and stand with me while I get a few of my things."

"And then? You have somewhere to go then?"

"Yes."

The policeman goes upstairs with me. My father is like a whole other person, back to that sinister calm self. "If you're going to arrest me, would you give me a moment to put on some clothes?" he says.

"One thing at a time now. Right now I'm just getting some information for a report. And the girl just wants to get a few things."

"You can't take her out of here. She is a child and she's under my control."

"Well, sir, according to her date of birth, it seems she just turned eighteen. Is that right?"

"Yes."

"That makes her an adult."

"In my country, the legal age of adulthood is twenty-one."

"I'm not sure how things are in your country, but in the United States she's an adult at eighteen and she can go wherever she wants."

I look around my room for things to put in my backpack. This time I know I'm really never coming back. But it feels good. I stuff in all the clothes I can fit. A few pictures. Nothing else matters. Everything else can be replaced.

Jose, big booger trails running out of his nose, walks over to his bed and hands me the SpongeBob pillow. He is in full post-sob hiccup mode. I feel like I should argue for him to keep it. But I really kind of want it. I kiss him on top of his head, tuck the pillow under my arm, look up at the beanpole cop. "I'm ready."

I give him Chelsea's address. Somehow he knows where it is.

"Hey, kiddo, you okay?"

"Yeah."

"You need to go to the hospital or something?"

"No."

"I've got two daughters, and I have to tell you, I don't under-stand how people can hurt children."

I smile at him. I try to imagine him out of uniform, at his daughters' sports games, a cheering father, not a potential threat with a nightstick and a gun and the phone number to the immigration authorities. He's huge, filling up the cop car, his head almost touching the roof of it. But his blue eyes aren't icy. They crinkle up around the edges, giving him an almost sweet air. His smile is very kind.

"I don't understand either," I say.

"But you know, you go out there and live a good life and don't worry about all that."

"I will."

"You call us if you need anything else, or a copy of the police report. Anything. You stay safe now."

"Thank you." He is nothing like what I thought he would be. He waits for the door to open before waving and driving away.

Chelsea's mother is the one who opens the door.

"M.T., are you okay?"

"I'm kind of not okay. Can I sleep over?"

"Of course."

"I mean . . . can I stay for more than just a night or two? Until I can find a place?"

"Tell me what happened."

And so, I do.

IT FEELS LIKE A NIGHT OF ENDINGS. WITH CHELSEA SLEEPING next to me, I fire up the laptop. I write a message to Nate:

"Hey, I just wanted to write and say thanks and sorry. Thanks for being a great boyfriend. Sorry for all the times I freaked out or seemed distant. One day I hope we can sit together and I'll be able to tell you the reasons why. I hope you're doing great."

I close my eyes and imagine where he might be in a few months. On campus somewhere, his freckles darker from his time on the boat, his room messy but not disastrous. I wonder if he wears the golf shirt I bought him, or if the gag copy of *Hamlet* I gave him still sits in his room at home. I let the smell of him wash over me, the *I love you* Post-its, the snuggling in his family room. It makes me a little sad, but mostly it makes me grateful. He came along and changed me, made me a better me. And maybe that's a pretty good reason for someone to be in your life, even if just for a little while.

CHAPTER THIRTY-FOUR

Since I'm usually at the park first, I sit on the back of a bench to wait. Always the same one. As soon as Jose sees me, he starts a full-on run and jumps up on the bench and onto me with such force that I'm afraid he's going to knock me down backward. My mom walks at the same pace the whole way, except when she's about ten steps away from the bench. Then she speeds up. We do double cheek kisses hello. I like that better than hugging.

We walk over to the playground slowly. Jose runs ahead of us, his pants looking a little like flood pants because he's grown two inches since the summer and his hair is long. I smell the brown acorn air—the crunchy leaves air—and know it is going to turn cold soon.

"You still have my SpongeBob pillow?" Jose asks every week.

"Yep, I sleep with it every night." Which sounds like a lie, except it's true.

"How are you?" asks my mother.

"I'm good. How about you guys?"

"We're fine."

I have decided that this is the week I'm going to tell her.

"I got into a college," I say.

"Did you? How wonderful! How?"

"Chelsea's mom helped me a little. I got financial aid. I'm going to start next January. It's . . . a college where you sleep away."

"How far?"

"Connecticut. A few hours' drive."

She sits down on the bench. Something crosses over her face. She tries to push it off with a smile.

Jose has heard this last part. "Where's Connecticut?" he asks. He's gripping my leg, playing with the hem of my shorts.

"Not too far," I say.

"Will you come visit me?"

"We'll see each other, of course. And if Mommy learns to email, I'll email you pictures."

"I told you you'd go to college," says my mom. A tear spills over the rim of her bottom eyelid and hangs there in her eyelash.

"Yeah, you're like some fortune teller or something. So what are you going to do?"

"I talked to the Nun and she told me about a place I can take my high school test. I'm studying for it now."

"And it's okay? With the no papers?"

"Yes."

Jose says, "Mommy is like you now, always reading books."

"I guess we won't see you much when you're in Connecticut," she says.

"I'll come home on vacations and summers. I mean, I won't come to the apartment, but I'll be around here."

"He doesn't hit anymore, since you're gone."

"I guess I was the trigger."

"That's not what I meant."

"I know."

"He's really sorry he got like that. If you were only in the apartment every once in a while, it might not be so bad."

"I can't. You know that."

"I do know, yes." She's quiet for a long time. She absently plays with a blade of grass Jose has picked for her.

She reaches in her purse, pulls out a roll of bills, and puts it in my hand.

"Are you into robbing banks now?" I ask.

"Since you've graduated the nuns are paying me. A little. And I'm sewing more. Here, take it."

"Why don't you go buy Jose some new clothes with it?"

"Don't worry about him. I've got it." She's quiet for a minute. Then she says, "Your father asked me to ask you to see him."

"Why?"

"I just think he wants to talk."

"I don't want to."

"I think you should."

"I don't want to hear his insults anymore."

"I think he'll be different this time. Just try. In a public place. Even if you just say good-bye to him."

"Okay."

"So when did you say you're leaving?" she says.

"January."

"So next week here then?"

"Every week until it gets too cold."

She puts her arms around me. I hug back. She says, "I don't think it will ever get too cold."

We sit like that, hugging, for a long time. She's stronger than I remember her being. Or maybe I didn't used to let her hug me. I bury my nose in the hair that falls down around her neck. She smells like picadillo, and the apartment, and every lullaby she ever sang me. But I won't let her see me cry.

She says, "This thing, you know. There are more important things than whether someone says you can have some papers and numbers. You're one of the strongest people I know. Way stronger than me. Step by step, you'll find the way. You're going to do amazing things."

"You too, I think."

"I think so, too." She takes my hand. I let her. "Let's walk together halfway."

CHAPTER THIRTY-FIVE

meet my father at the coffee shop where I caught him reading instead of working. He's got a cup of coffee in front of him. He stands up when I get there. I sit across from him.

"So," he says.

"Here we are."

"You never came back."

"No."

"You still wear too much eyeliner."

He says it sheepishly, like he's trying to make a joke and it's the only one that occurs to him. Like he's trying to call up a shared memory, but the only ones he's coming up with are the ones when he says things like, "You wear too much eyeliner."

"So . . ." I say, my eyes steady on him.

"I just . . ." He lifts up his chest, breathes in deep, like he's screwing up courage. "About that night."

"Yeah?"

"I don't know . . . I don't know how we got here."

"You hit me. That's how we got here."

"No, I mean . . ." He looks like he gives up trying to explain, is quiet for too long a beat, and moves on to another approach. "You know, when you were born, I felt guilty."

"Why?"

"I just held you and I had never felt anything like that feeling. I was just some snot-nosed kid. All I'd ever cared about was hanging out with my friends, looking cool. But you . . . you looked just like me, but in tiny baby form. It was the most amazing thing. I felt guilty. I knew I would never be able to love your mother the way that I loved you."

I don't know what to say to this. Luckily, I don't have to say anything. He's on a roll. "It wasn't supposed to be like this. I was supposed to come to this country alone. You know that? Work and send money back home to your mother."

"Why didn't you?"

"Because you came along and I couldn't leave you."

"So it's my fault."

"No, that's not . . ." I know it's not what he means, but I enjoy making it difficult for him. So many times when I was little and he would hit me, I would close my eyes to fight back the tears by thinking to myself, "One day I'll be big and strong and you'll be old and weak." He isn't exactly old and weak yet, but is that white hair by his temple? And I'm not big and strong, at least not in the way that I dreamed I would be one day. But I'm not small and weak, either.

"That's not what I mean," he repeats. "You changed the plans, yes. But I was glad you did. So we all came together. We were only supposed to be here six months, to save money."

"But it didn't work out that way."

"You were so precious. We both knew right away that the plan of your mother and I both getting jobs would never work. We couldn't leave you with strangers. And then . . . the time goes by so fast in this country. Everything is sped up."

"Stop saying 'this country.' This is *my* country."

"But it's not. That's what you don't understand. One day when you're older, you'll understand."

"I don't think I'll ever see it that way."

"This country was just a detour. It's like a detour that won't end. But it wasn't supposed to be this way. You talking like them. You saying you wouldn't go back home. You always worry that *they* don't want *us*. But it's *us* who shouldn't want *them*. They put their old people in old age homes to die alone. All they care about is money. We're not like them. Don't you see?"

"No." We are on two sides of a big canyon, screaming as loud as we can, but barely getting our messages over to each other.

"You should come home," he says.

"You said you were going to kill me. You did more than say it."

"I never would have let it get that far."

"I should have had you arrested."

He looks out the window. "If you had, maybe I'd be home by now. Maybe that wouldn't be so bad after all. You should come home. You think the brave thing is running away. The brave thing is facing the problems."

"The way *you* do?"

"Better than me, I hope."

"I'm not coming home. But what about them? Mami? Joey? What's it going to be like for them?" I want to hear him say he won't turn his anger on them now.

"You think I don't learn anything. And maybe I don't, who knows? But something broke inside your mother the day you left. It's over with us, I think. Anyway, I can't . . . I don't know how to explain it to you. But I won't do that to them."

"People like you don't change."

"Probably not," he says. "Too proud. Too stubborn. But the world changes around us, keeps on going without us. That's how it is with your mother. I don't count anymore. You were the last person I could ever hope to—You'll have kids one day and you'll see. There will be one that is just like you, and you'll do anything to make her come out perfect, to not grow crooked. One day when you're older, you'll understand." It's like if he says it enough times, maybe he'll believe it. He looks so sad and tired. And for the first time, small. And I feel strong for realizing that maybe I will never understand. That I will always have my own separate truth that no one can ever change.

Then he says, "You used to take money out of my wallet, right?"

I look at him, not at the spot on his forehead I've been looking at to keep from making eye contact but, for the first time, right in his eyes. I am shocked that he knew all along, that he's saying something now. I feel a deep shame. Not that he knew, but that I once was the kind of person who stole.

"Yes."

"Why?"

"That money you took out of my notebook. You owed it to me."

"How much was it?"

"A hundred and seventy-five dollars."

"How much were you able to get back?"

"Sixty-two."

He reaches into his pants pocket, takes out his wallet, pulls it open, grabs a twenty. "This is all I have. I'll send the rest with your mother, a little at a time."

I don't know which is worse, that he's only got twenty dollars, or that he's offering his last twenty dollars to me.

"It's okay," I say, pushing his hand back. He looks at me a long time, then puts the bill back in his wallet.

327

CHAPTER THIRTY-SIX

Chelsea's mom comes into the family room where Chelsea and I are eating popcorn and watching that reality show about the swimsuit model who marries the little person.

"Turn on CNN," she says to Chelsea.

"What?"

"The president just made an executive decision on DREAMers. Teenagers who were brought over here when they were kids, like you, M."

"What does that mean?"

"I'm not even sure yet. When I saw the headline online I just came in here."

We switch the channel. I catch it just in time to hear a part of the president's speech. He's saying, "Now, let's be clear—this is not amnesty, this is not immunity. This is not a path to citizenship. It's not a permanent fix. This is a temporary stopgap measure that lets us focus our resources wisely while giving a degree of relief and hope to talented, driven, patriotic young people."

Talented. Driven. Patriotic. The words echo in my chest. I try them on, wondering if they could apply to me. I decide they do.

They end the clip of the president and go to a news anchor, a woman with perfect blond hair and huge glow-in-the-dark teeth and a whole lot of eye makeup.

"There you have it, the president making his historic announcement today, issuing a politically charged policy directive that will make about eight hundred thousand young people who were brought in to the country illegally as children safe from deportation proceedings, and may make them eligible for work permits."

Chelsea mutes the TV. I keep watching the anchor with the tons of eye makeup talking on the screen on mute. Next to her in a box they show an image of a baby, then some students holding a sign saying, 'No human being is illegal.' And finally the president again.

"This doesn't help my mom," I say.

"No. I think it's only for people who were sixteen or younger when they came over."

"She was twenty-two."

"So no."

"But my brother is okay."

"Where was he born?"

"Here. Mid-Bergen."

"So he's a citizen."

"This means college and a work permit for me, but no citizenship," I say.

"For now," says Chelsea's mom. "But it reminds me what Martin Luther King said about justice. Do you know the quote?"

"No."

"'The arc of the moral universe is long, but it bends towards justice.'"

"I like that. The start of the arc." I smile.

I close my eyes, for the first time in a long time not wading a lake of silence. The future begins to take a color in my mind. And it shines.

AUTHOR'S NOTE

I was "illegal" like M.T. once. The Immigration Control and Reform Act of 1986 put me on a path to eventual citizenship and changed my life in every way imaginable. I spent many dark and lonely years wondering what the future might hold for me. Now I wake up every morning grateful for the opportunity to have a life I love in the only country I've ever called home. I always like to joke that you never love your country as much as when you've grown up being afraid you'd get kicked out of it. M.T.'s story is very much like mine, but very much her own, too.

Besides her uncertain immigration status, there are other serious issues that M.T. faces. One is domestic violence. Her dad is abusive for his own hard-to-understand and complicated reasons. Like many kids who are abused, M.T. spends a lot of time hating herself and wondering what she did wrong. It affects all her relationships, not just the one with her father. It's common but misguided. The abused is never to blame. If you or anyone you know is facing a situation like that, the important thing is to reach out for help from a trusted adult. There are also organizations that can help, and they're listed at the end of this note.

The other issue she grapples with is suicide. Contemplating suicide is a common if extreme way to cope with situations that feel hopeless. According to a study from the U.S. Substance Abuse and Mental Health Services administration, thirteen percent of teens between the ages of fourteen and seventeen have seriously considered suicide. It doesn't make you weird or wrong to try to think of all the ways out of a situation that hurts. I thought about it for years in my teens and twenties. It was isolating and sad. Now, decades into the happy life that came after all the pain,

I realize what a drastic and permanent solution that would have been. It would have prevented everything wonderful I have now. I know now that it always gets better. *Always*. If you or someone you know is thinking about suicide, reach out for help immediately.

How can you tell if someone is "just trying to get attention" or seriously contemplating suicide? You can't. It sounds and looks the same. (And I would argue that if someone is trying to get attention by threatening suicide, they still need someone to talk to.) Reach out for help anyway, even if your friend gets mad at you. Alive and mad is better than dead.

Lastly, I want to make sure you understand that this is a fictional story. The way things work out in it *could* have happened that way— M.T.'s dad could have just stopped being physically abusive and she could have come to understand that suicide is not the answer. But in real life, you never know how things are going to go. So if you or a friend are in similar situations, don't try to fix it alone or by hoping things will get better. Make your own happy ending by reaching out for help and tapping into all the love and support around you. Even on your darkest day, when you don't see it or believe in it, it's everywhere. Believe me. Just the fact that you can hold this book in your hand and that I was around to write it at all is proof of just how magical and unexpected life can be.

RESOURCES

For victims of domestic violence

National Domestic Violence Hotline—www.thehotline.org

For suicide prevention

The Society for the Prevention of Teen Suicide—www.sptsusa.org

TEEN Nineline Suicide and Crisis Hotline—1-800-786-2929

For more domestic violence and suicide resources, as well as more of my own story, go to mariaeandreu.com/tssoe_resources.

ACKNOWLEDGMENTS

I have always loved acknowledgments pages. Back when I was in the darkest hours of my teen years, undocumented, unsure about the future, books were the wonderful place I could go to be free. I always read the acknowledgments pages with awe. How did writers, those magical creatures, surround themselves with so many special people? I was so alone, so "not good enough," I couldn't imagine what luck that must take.

Now, all these years later, I find myself daunted by the task of listing all the people who supported me in the creation of this book. Like all the authors I admire, I too am surrounded by an amazing cast of characters. If I omit one, it is strictly a function of limited space and flagging memory.

First, to everyone who guided me on my journey from aspiring writer to published author. To Miss Bordiga, best English teacher ever, a heart full of gratitude. I would not have pursued a writing career had you not been my teacher. I know that flights of angels sing thee to thy rest. To everyone at Holy Rosary, a school that now only lives in our imaginations, thanks for four wonderful and wacky years. Norah Alberto and Marcela Sotomayor, Fido sisters, my Chelseas, thanks for a lifetime of friendship. And for the real-life Nate, thanks for being such a wonderful first boyfriend. Jim Warnke, thanks for all the surrogate fathering and for shining a door on the way out. Michael Falvey, my favorite sheepdog: without you I never would have made it through all the doubts to the other side. Your love and support made this dream possible.

Romano L. Mazzoli and Alan K. Simpson, thank you for the 1986 immigration reform bill that paved the way for the life I know today.

Charles Salzberg and Susan Shapiro, amazing writing teachers and human beings, thank you. To every agent and editor who rejected me, thank you for helping me get strong and determined. (No, really, I mean it. I needed to get rejected until the day when I was ready not to be.) To the agent whose name is lost to me who first suggested at the Backspace pitch conference that my book wanted to be a young adult novel, a million thank yous. Laurie Halse Anderson who helped me see just how beautiful YA could be. Bergen County Writers Group: Hans Spiegel, Betsy Voreacos, Alyson Raskin, Janet Blair, Christian K., and Pat Kinney and all the others who have passed through, thank you for being way too kind about my writing. Deborah Bigelow and the rest of your crew, you rock.

Ellie Spiegel and Margaret White and every other loving soul at the Community of Friends in Action, all my gratitude for showing me what compassion and activism mean and for helping to show me that the arc of the moral universe really does bend toward justice. Wythe Boehm, my "replacement Pablo," for always asking to read the manuscript even though you and I both know you can write better. Oh, and for marrying the inimitable Rebecca Nemec, future agriculture secretary or world ruler or whatever else she decides to be. And for being crazy enough to think that I could write a wedding ceremony.

Genevieve Gagne-Hawes, seeing your gorgeous name pop up in my inbox telling me you'd pulled me out of the slush pile remains one of the highlights of my life. Ken Wright, your first email to me still sits framed in my living room. My wonderful agent, Susan Cohen, the soul of patience and business savvy, a basketful full of thanks and chocolate. Brianne Johnson and every other magical person at Writers House, I hope you know how much of a dream come true you guys really are. My wise and smart editor at Running Press, Lisa Cheng, thank you for your indefatigable slaying of all the awful "oh my Gods" and "wells" in my original manuscript and for asking all the questions that made the story better. Your belief in me and your gentle guidance have made this a perfect experience.

And . . . is it weird to acknowledge a house? I spent a lot of time being afraid that I would be homeless or, at least, country-less. When I finally found you, my beautiful little colonial, I knew right away I wanted to belong to you. For letting me feel so safe and so connected to one spot of earth and for giving me a peaceful spot to write my stories, house, I love you. Even though I didn't meet you until I was twenty-nine years old, you're definitely the house that I grew up in. My wonderful town, the "Athens of New Jersey," thanks for being full of the kinds of people and places I always wanted to know.

Finally, to my family. How does one adequately give thanks for a lifetime of love? To La Mami for the late-night sewing and the maté and all the times you figured out how to persevere through impossible situations. Thank you, Pablo, brother extraordinaire, for being the coolest and smartest person I know. I look forward to blurbing your book soon.

And my children: my beloved Andreanna, how your eight-year-old's reaction blew my mind when I finally got the courage to tell you my story. And how your belief in me kept me going even when I didn't believe in myself! Thanks for painting me into a corner by telling every teacher you've had since the third grade that your mother is an author, even when I still kind of wasn't. And my Zachary, thank you for your sweetness and goodness and your admirable example of single-mindedly going after your goals. Thank you both for choosing me as your mother in that mystical realm where souls choose moms. When you came along, I finally got it.

8/14, 12/16, 12/17, 4/19